In Search of Lost Time

Conversation Pieces

A Small Paperback Series from Aqueduct Press
Subscriptions available: www.aqueductpress.com

About the Aqueduct Press Conversation Pieces Series

The feminist engaged with sf is passionately interested in challenging the way things are, passionately determined to understand how everything works. It is my constant sense of our feminist-sf present as a grand conversation that enables me to trace its existence into the past and from there see its trajectory extending into our future. A genealogy for feminist sf would not constitute a chart depicting direct lineages but would offer us an ever-shifting, fluid mosaic, the individual tiles of which we will probably only ever partially access. What could be more in the spirit of feminist sf than to conceptualize a genealogy that explicitly manifests our own communities across not only space but also time?

Aqueduct's small paperback series, Conversation Pieces, aims to both document and facilitate the "grand conversation." The Conversation Pieces series presents a wide variety of texts, including short fiction (which may not always be sf and may not necessarily even be feminist), essays, speeches, manifestoes, poetry, interviews, correspondence, and group discussions. Many of the texts are reprinted material, but some are new. The grand conversation reaches at least as far back as Mary Shelley and extends, in our speculations and visions, into the continually-created future. In Jonathan Goldberg's words, "To look forward to the history that will be, one must look at and retell the history that has been told." And that is what Conversation Pieces is all about.

L. Timmel Duchamp

Jonathan Goldberg, "The History That Will Be" in Louise
    Fradenburg and Carla Freccero, eds., *Premodern Sexualities* (New
    York and London: Routledge, 1996)

Conversation Pieces
Volume 56

To Lisa, Hope you enjoy! Karen Heuler

In Search of Lost Time

by
Karen Heuler

Published by Aqueduct Press
PO Box 95787
Seattle, WA 98145-2787
www.aqueductpress.com

10 9 8 7 6 5 4 3 2 1
ISBN: 978-1-61976-125-4

Cover illustrations: Mannequin, © Can Stock Photo Inc. /
Robert Schneider; Background, © Can Stock Photo Inc. /
alexzaitsev; Clock face, © Can Stock Photo Inc. / pdesign

Original Block Print of Mary Shelley by Justin Kempton:
www.writersmugs.com

Printed in the USA by Applied Digital Imaging

She had been an idiot to hope for good news. Hildy realized this as the doctor's words droned on. When you were young, good news moved in big and little waves; that's what youth was. But she was forty-seven. Still long and lean, still striding hard. Still wearing tight tight pants and soft boots with kitten heels. She liked to lead with her legs; she liked the idea of them rounding corners before the rest of her did. She painted the heels of her boots red.

So, cancer. Hildy stared as the doctor patiently explained how the process worked. Of course there would be a process for it. She was fine with process.

Cancer of the Tempora—who had ever heard of that? Not quite an organ, part of the brain, exactly the spot where the body experienced time. So, basically, her little lapses, gaps, fugues—all of it a disease with time. It could kill her (well, something would, eventually) but in strange stages. Her body could be healthy except for this, but something might age so fast that it would stop working right, within a week or a year, hard to judge, unless she had treatment.

And so she had treatment. She was going to be a survivor.

When they hooked her up for chemo, though, she had an unexpected reaction. Sitting there, in the comfy large adjustable chair with the hinged flat armrests, she saw a change in the air around her. Mists enveloped people, vapors with colors. When they walked, the mists moved with them, like gauzy hajibs. She blinked, rubbed her eyes, then called the nurse.

"My eyes are fuzzy. I can't get them clear," she said, leaning forward slightly.

"Any nausea? Itching? Do you feel weak or dizzy?"

"No; nothing. But my eyesight—"

The nurse checked her line, tapped the chemo bag. "No one's reported any side-effect like that before, but there's always a first time. Is it getting worse?"

"No. Yes. I think I'm getting used to it. Never mind." Hildy leaned back. She was a strong woman, not a wimp. And her eyesight actually wasn't worse, just different. It wasn't blurry, for instance; it was merely…deeper.

She kept looking at the empty chair next to her. She tried not to picture Noah's face—the wide-open grin, the brown eyes with a humorous squint, the fuzzy hair he forced to be ruly. He liked the word *unruly,* and he liked to play with it. "I see," he once said, "you're being ruly today." And he had turned his head, twisted it upside down. "Did you know we're incapable of recognizing faces upside down? You could put your own head upside down and not be able to pick it out."

"Why would I want to pick out my head upside down?" she had protested. She had enjoyed that kind of thing.

The drugs made her head feel full, but that mist, that aura, stayed faintly present. She felt thick and slow, so she stared at the tints that hung around the nurses and the patients. When visitors came, they brought their colors with them; no one was excluded.

She went home and lay down for a few days. After the nausea left, she went back to work teaching basic computer skills. It was an adult ed class run out of a high school. Some of the students were old and lonely; some were out of work and hoping to add to their resume. She saw thin mists around them, except for a young man who'd dropped out of college. His aura was thick; when she passed by him she tended to leave more space.

And then, vaguely—was it deliberate?—she put her hand in his aura, twisted it around, trying to make it look like a normal action. She cupped her hand in it, pulled the mist toward her. It felt heavy, a little oily, like lemon oil. It soothed the skin of her palm and gave her a sensation of youthful indifference, as if everything worked well without thinking.

She inhaled it.

The student, Joey, noticed something different and looked at her with raised eyebrows, but she moved on, breathing deeply.

She sat down at her desk, feeling her heart beat steadily, feeling her lungs moving without an ache. She felt a light skipping in her chest, a pleasant anticipation, as if anything could happen at any moment. Was this some sudden new side-effect of chemo? It didn't feel like it. But it was unexpected, and intoxicating.

She kept glancing at Joey as she went through the lesson for the day. The students dutifully bent their heads and followed along, creating a file structure on their computers. As she went around the class, checking their work, she leant over Joey and breathed in heavily. His neck turned red, and he looked up at her. "I get dizzy," she apologized.

They knew about her illness; they loved her for it.

For the next class, she saved a take-out coffee cup and lid and pretended she needed the caffeine, that coffee worked somewhat like smelling salts. She made her way around the room, keeping her eye on Joey. She took the lid off the coffee, pretending to blow on it. He looked up at her quickly, smiled, his eyes looking kind, and when he turned back to his work, she made a quick pass over his head, lifted the cup to her face and took a gulp. Again that feeling, that inner sense that all was well, and it overwhelmed the knowledge that she had cancer, pushed it away like a tide so it was gone. In its own way, it was similar to the efforts at visualizing triumph over cancer, which the nurses had advised her to do. She found it hard to imagine cancer, in fact, and if indeed she did have cancer she was sure—body-sure—that it was weak and could be overcome. She wanted to run or flirt or laugh instead; that was the right thing to do. She was strong and supple, and she wanted a hamburger.

As a test, she continued down the row and swooped her cup in the thin mist near her oldest student and sniffed. Some of the exhilaration left and a greater sense of dutifulness hit her. And a worry about money, which was new.

She thought about this after class was over and after repeated sniffs at the coffee cup resulted in nothing but lightheadedness.

She asked Anne, the chemo nurse, if there was any advantage to hanging around young people when you had cancer. The nurse laughed. "Can't stand them myself," she said cheerfully (all the cancer nurses were cheerful). "You have to be half my age now to be considered young!" She shook her head and laughed.

Hildy could see that: Anne's aura was almost as thin as her own.

She glanced down at her own hand, studying the differences in aura between it and the nurse's hand. Anne didn't notice, so Hildy's question had raised no obvious concerns. Sometimes it was hard to know what to discuss, what to focus on. The country of cancer had its own borders, its own language, and surely its own laws. She had entered strange territory.

She knew she would be sick after chemo, no matter what medication they gave her for nausea. She'd told Anne that she'd gotten sick after the first round, and Anne suggested some Eastern medicine might counter the fatigue that followed the nausea. "Keep all roads open," Anne said cheerfully as she handed her a business card for an acupuncturist. "You never know what will help."

O tempora, O mores!, Hildy thought, as she hurried to get home before the vomiting started. Go to an acupuncturist for needles to change the effects of the needle the chemo nurse gave her! That was called irony, though it seemed like sarcasm.

Two days later, when her stomach settled, she went in search of the acupuncturist on the business card. She stalked Chinatown—down Mott Street, past Catherine Street—and stopped at a storefront on Wey Street. The store was some steps down, below street level, and the lettering was along the upper edge of the window. "Unusual medicines," it said. "To heal and strengthen unusual things."

Hildy was charmed by the words. She walked down the steps and opened the door to a small room with a deep rug and pillowy chairs. A man came out from one of two doors at the back. He nodded and walked over to a desk to the right, where he adjusted some papers and then motioned her to come forward and sit down. There was a chair off to the side of his desk, and she took it. He gazed at her mildly.

She waited for him to speak, and when he didn't, she finally said, "I see auras."

"Many do," he replied, nodding once. "Is this a problem for you?"

"Actually, it's physical. I don't just see them, I can take some of them." She waited for his reaction.

He looked at her keenly, bit his lower lip for a moment, then clasped his hands together. "I've heard of this. It's a very rare gift. Now that you can see auras, it's possible for you to learn what they mean."

She sighed and relaxed. "I thought they meant something. At first I was worried that it was a problem with my eyes." She hesitated. "Or my mind."

He had her fill out a card with her name and address and diagnosis, then silently motioned her to follow him to the next room. He turned on a tape of flute music that sounded like water running down a mountainside—very nice.

"Just loosen your clothing so nothing constricts, and lie down on your back on the table." She did so.

"Lie very still," he said, his back turned to her as he sorted through his needles. "You have the ability to see things, so think of a place that's soothing and harmonious."

She thought of sleep, the only peaceful thing in her life. Though maybe she should worry that she wouldn't wake? She never did worry; she loved sleep and all the relief it provided. He placed the needles quickly, a tiny touch and then a tap. She felt herself relax. She took off her scarf, and he tapped needles into her bald head. Slight tap, move on. Slight tap, move on. It never hurt.

After he had placed all the needles, he lowered the lights and left the room. The music became a little louder and then softer. At first she lay there listening for him, trying to figure out if he'd gone back to his chair behind the desk, if he'd gone out the door to the street, if there was another room where he stood, waiting for her session to end. What did it matter what he did? He could stand wherever he chose. She dozed off.

When he turned the lights on again, she felt calm and refreshed. She had to remind herself that there was still chemo in her veins, and chemo ahead, and that a few minutes of therapeutic ease weren't a cure. She listened as he told her she would be free of nausea if she came to him before each treatment, that she would feel whole and healthy, that the tumors would grow weak and be unable to fight back.

"I have a special relationship with cancer patients," he said as she paid him. "I know I can help. I suffer myself from a violent temper—perhaps you noticed the small needle in my ear lobe? It keeps me calm. I only tell you this so you'll know how I trust the needles absolutely. Would you like to schedule another appointment?"

She would wait and see how she felt. She was certainly relaxed; she had to admit that. That heavy feeling, that strange taste she had at the back of her throat—well, it was there but she didn't feel obliged to think about it. She walked slowly to the subway, looking at people and their mists. Some auras floated like seaweed around people; others were more static. Maybe that meant nothing.

By the time she reached her apartment, she was starting to wobble a little. Her eyelids dragged; her mouth dragged; she took off her boots and crawled into bed. She wished, more than anything, to have Noah beside her. She wanted to have his hand on her head, stroking her forehead, telling her the exhaustion would pass, the bad feelings would pass.

In a few days, she felt strong again and wrapped her head in a scarf, penciled in some eyebrows, pulled on her boots, and went to the park.

It was a sunny day. The air was cool, but that just made it a pleasure to wear a sweater.

For the first time, she noticed that the dogs had colors around them, too. Little doggie auras. Draping them, like a bright second coat of fur.

What were those colors? What did it all mean? People usually had the same general array of tints, but then she'd pass someone with a predominant color—salmon or spring green—and she'd wonder what the differences between people meant. She smiled at herself. They meant the differences between people! Whatever the reason, she felt buoyant. She studied the auras more closely and could see that the colors were held in place by a webbing of a translucent pearlish color. Like a mosaic. Colors, either large or small, held by strands of pearl. What were those strands? What were those colors?

She passed the dog runs and strolled into the swing area, the kiddie playgrounds with their benches surrounding the sandpile and the teeter-totter. She began to chat up the nannies, who were leaning over babies with almost white auras, and she took deep breaths because she assumed she would feel as good as she had when she sniffed Joey, but then the nannies began eying her.

No one knows this, but I know it, she thought. All these people have youth or health or something spraying out of them or trying to get in—however it works, it's information of some kind, and no one else sees it.

No one else could see what she could see.

She smiled fondly on all of them. She nodded at the nannies and looked with interest as their colored halos slopped back and forth just a twitch delayed. If nothing else, it was pretty. But it must be something else. In the midst of her ordeal, it was a gift she hadn't yet opened.

She spent the next few days with her multi-colored scarf wrapped around her head like a turban. She penciled in eyebrows with different colors on different days. She took large steps when she walked in her calf-high boots with the little red heels, so her legs would pivot out like a windmill.

⟋

Once upon a time she had been in love and happy. Not totally happy—Noah was married—but she had pushed aside her own moral qualms and decided to take what she could get, which was this good thing, this happiness with Noah. At times she wondered if Noah was faithful to her—an awful, stupid question. Even when Noah was gone, was elsewhere, she still loved him. Wasn't occasional love better than no love?

It was. It had been.

⟋

She bought a small backpack and then some jars and bottles with snap-on lids to make collecting auras easy. She had a purpose and a curiosity. That, plus the turban and the missing eyebrows and the calf-high boots with red heels, made her feel empowered.

Though people began to notice her and her containers. It was harder to hang around a park and scoop a jar near a baby; it caught people's eyes and once or twice someone got up to approach her, but she scooted off.

At the playground one day she noticed a man with a bottle mustache standing in the pervert spot, under a tree and behind a bush behind the fence at the playground. It was interesting, how she could see who was aware of whom; the nannies clustered together, making a solid wall between the pervert and the kids. The occasional dad came in, and the nannies shifted, the pervert vanished. She knew when they had their eyes on her as well, no child in sight, strange-looking, booted no matter the weather.

The next time she went, the pervert stepped out from a tree and faced her insolently. He wore a derby, and his mustache looked fake, close up. There was something else…

"I know what you're doing," he hissed.

"Do you?" she asked faintly. Her heart ticked faster, but the trick was never to volunteer what she was doing: he was probably guessing, and possibly guessing wrong.

"You're stealing time," he said. "I can see it. You and your bottles and jars."

Her eyes widened. Her hand automatically reached backwards to her pack, which he noted. She could almost see him think about grabbing it and running. But he decided against it.

She took off her backpack and took out a jar. They were all empty that day; she had merely opened and closed jars while the nannies had their eyes on her. She didn't yet have a system. She offered him a jar. "This?" she asked. "This is an empty jar. I collect them."

He grabbed the jar. "Whose time is this?" he asked.

Her heart took a sickening lurch, but she hid it. She had begun to have suspicions about what those auras meant, and this confirmed it. So those auras were time, clean and overflowing from the youngest, with lots of space to fill in, but getting more lurid, more crowded, year by lived year.

And he can't tell it's empty, she noted. He can't tell.

"That one was weak," she said, taking it from him. She said it as a test, to see what he knew. "So that's what it is. Time. I see auras. This was from an old man, very weak, you won't want it."

He stepped back a little, blowing air out of his mouth and nose noisily. "Don't do that!" he hissed. "Don't get involved with weak time. It can wear you down even faster."

"How do you know this?" she asked. "Who else knows? And how did you find out?"

He was calculating how much he would need to reveal; she could see various answers occurring to him and being discarded. What difference did it make? Why would he hide what it meant? He'd already given her the information that mattered. The aura she saw was actually time; she was stealing it when she ran her cup through the mist around people; and there was a difference in quality of time; all these things she now knew. What else was there?

She lifted a jar to his aura, feeling it, and he jumped back. "I know what that means," he said. "And you're not taking it from me, not one minute, not one second."

She stiffened. "*Taking* it from you," she repeated slowly.

"Of course." He laughed harshly, his mustache bobbing up and down, his rubbery face producing lines that lifted up his cheeks. "If you remove something, there's less of it at the source, no? Isn't that a law of physics or something?"

She had stolen time from Joey! How could that be true? She liked Joey; she didn't want to harm him; she didn't want to harm anyone. She had been curious. Was it terrible to be curious? She swallowed painfully. "How much time have I taken?"

His eyes were dark and bright, and she felt a kind of interest coming from them. He found her interesting—what, her stupidity? Was that amusing?

"Depends on the container," he answered finally. His eyes slid down to the jar she held. "Probably only minutes with that—don't you feel how long it affects you? Can't you tell?"

She hadn't noticed how long it was; she had been so struck by that brief feeling of health and buoyancy and youth. Joey's minutes, she now knew. A brief visit to his life.

It had been so vivid. If it was only minutes, what harm would come of getting a few more from him—or from the babies in the playground, or anyone? It was just a minute or two. Her eyes drifted away from him, and when they came back to his odd face with what must be, she was absolutely certain, a fake mustache, she saw him glinting at her, his teeth showing between his lips.

"What's the harm?" he asked. "Just a little bit here and there. No one will even miss it. And I can find a market for you." He had a sly, artificial smile. "We can work together on this." He held out his hand. "Michael P, that's what everyone calls me. P for Pleasant? Profitable? Nicknames can be tricky."

"Hildy," she said.

He nodded, as if he already knew that. "Well, Hildy, you have a special talent. Not everyone can do what you can do. I, for instance, can see a little of what you see, but I can't touch it. There are others, of course, who are like you. They're not all honorable or nice, so you have those sudden deaths of athletes and so on—their hours emptied out so there was nothing left. I'm sure you wouldn't do that. Enough of that, and people are bound to get suspicious. But there's a market for time. There are people who are down to their own last hours, and they'll pay plenty to have some more, a mix of hours will work, boys and girls and young and not-so-young. I can get you connected with the market. It would take you years to do anything on your own. And not everyone is so easy to work with!"

Someone had once told Hildy that you could tell if someone was lying by watching their ears. She hadn't been told what to watch for—but she looked at Michael P's ears and knew he was lying, though not what he was lying about. He lifted a hand to touch his ear when he saw her looking there.

He took his hand down. "What do you say?"

"I don't know. You've given me something to think about. I didn't even know what it all meant, and now I have to figure out what to do about it. If what you're saying is true."

His own eyes looked at the absence of her eyebrows. "Of course it's true. You can steal as many healthy hours as you please for yourself. And you can be rich. Rich and healthy. Not so bad."

If he was lying, though, maybe he was lying about stealing time. Maybe it wasn't as bad as it sounded; maybe he was trying to frighten her. At the back of her mind, too, there was a little voice reminding her that she might need the time, eventually. It was hard to have cancer and be noble.

And if she just took a little bit, she wouldn't really harm anyone. Who would miss a few minutes?

~

Hildy told herself it would be foolish to make a decision without knowing how much was true. She would have to run tests, so she got more jars from the store: jars with flip lids, press-on lids; she figured even screw-ons would work, but the jars themselves had to be lightweight and silent. No noisy snapping or popping to get anyone's attention. She had a feeling that there were both truth and lies in what Michael P said, and she had to find out for herself.

She made some experimental runs. She took time from people on lines, from people waiting for buses, from people picking up children after school, from the children on their way home, from cashiers as they lowered their heads, once from the combined aura of a couple kissing on a park bench. She labeled them with quick notes about where she found them.

And found this out: for a little while, she understood French; she couldn't stop thinking about horses; she felt like running and skipping; she felt aroused; she felt like crying. Each jar contained not only time but the associations of time. And she found, too, that hours held memories, and she would be suddenly stricken by losses or buoyed by joys, or desperately, paralyzingly worried or fearful for very good reasons. The hours were not clean, nor could she tell where the good hours in any person's life were, at least not yet. She started labeling where she had filled the jars—from the left side, right, front, back—hoping there was a system to it, an organizing principle.

Some sniffs had more of a story to them; some had more of a mood.

She had sniffed one jar and found herself remembering she was two months behind on rent, which wasn't true. But she had reached for her checkbook; she would have to learn to separate what the jars did from her own thoughts.

Some of the donor's memories were sharp and some were well-worn.

She had rows of jars now in her living room and masses of notes about what she was figuring out. She tried to sniff only half a jar so she could label their usefulness, but it was hard to open a lid and not have it all spill upwards, so she got jars with nozzles and spouts, and was a bit more successful. And she tried to hold two jars at once as she collected time, so she could test one and label the other. A large jar and a small jar.

It was hard to be inconspicuous.

She was stopped once or twice by suspicious people on the street, and a young man knocked a jar out of her hand when he turned and found her waving it behind him (because the aura was all around people, it was much safer to fill it behind their backs). She began to switch most of her research to the evening or the night, but the quality of the time she got then was different. She found that the jars she filled in the middle of the night had a torpid texture to them, a sense of waiting, a drawing in of the self. They were syrupy. She called them gray time, and they were immobilizing. If she sniffed one, she had to sit and wait it out. These hours seemed slow and sticky. Nothing productive could happen in gray time, the hours that felt the most isolated, the most dreaded.

So did auras shift depending on time of day?

She came home one day to find some of her jars missing. She knew exactly how many she had and where they were. To find five gone made her heart thud.

She looked out her window, down to the street, and there was Michael P across the street, looking up at her. He nodded, crossed the street, and buzzed her apartment. She let him up.

He looked over at the row of bottles and then held up a plastic shopping bag, lumpy with jars. "I thought that would get your attention," he said with satisfaction. "I can pay you for these, you know. I can steal them or I can pay you for them. Which is to say—we can work together or we can work against each other. I can be a good friend," he added, lowering his bag and his voice. "I can help you get whatever you need, whenever you need it."

She thought of the latest scan she'd had, showing that the cancer seemed to be receding. Were the scans good because she'd sniffed good time before she had them? She frowned. Were the jars of time influencing her mind *and* her body—suggesting things to her or changing her? Could she accidentally sniff the jars of a man who didn't yet know he was dying, and therefore take a little of his dying and mix it in with hers?

She asked Michael P about it and he shrugged. "Whatever you take, you're *adding* to your own hours. As long as you don't take the hour, the minute, the second someone dies, you'll experience that stolen hour and move on. It won't change what you have. But of course, there have been no *experiments* on this; no research. As the medical profession says, we rely on anecdotal evidence." He smirked.

She had two rows of jars on a table in her living room; he ran his hand along the tops of the jars. "I like the labels," he said. "Very helpful." He picked one up and read it. "8:30 p.m. Young man; drunk. Pleasant."

"And he hadn't seemed drunk at first," she said. "But he twirled around when I passed him and stumbled. Would it make me drunk if I tried it?" She resented Michael P's intrusion, but she was desperate for information. She had to ask, whether she could trust him or not. She would have to tally what he said against her own impressions.

"Depends on whether you grabbed the present hour," he said. "Our hours are mixed all around us, the hours we've lived. We hold on to them. Though I wonder if an Alzheimer's patient has true hours or imagined hours stuck around her. I met one who always seemed to be in a dream."

"How do you know about this? I never knew about this."

He smirked. "It's like a secret club, with a secret sign. Only a few people have your gift. Of course, there are entry points, and cancer treatment is one of them. The cells in your head get changed and distort perception—revealing things the healthy cells can't sense. Some hallucinogens will do it, but it's temporary, and not everyone believes what they see." He shrugged. "If it wears off then of course they ignore it. But there are a few people who test it out, the way you did. A bunch of us keep our eyes open; I was lucky enough to see you at it."

"And if I gave you jars, how would you pay me?"

"Oh, I'd give you some money. Say, five dollars a jar? Look at what you've already got—" His hand swept the table—"just in this room alone."

It wasn't even much of an offer. If she counted it all up, she'd have maybe a hundred dollars and an uneasy feeling. "I may need the time myself," she said finally. She might as well call it *time* even if she wasn't sure about it. She might as well play on his terms.

"You can always get more, can't you? And I have no doubt you'll grab and sniff whenever you take some time; like taking samples at a supermarket, no? Isn't that what you women do?" He was getting impatient; he started opening doors and drawers, looking for more bottles.

"Stop that," she said sharply.

He spun around to her. "If we're to work together, I have to know what you've been up to. And we'll work together," he said. "You need me. I can help you."

"I don't need any help. And did you know how thin your aura is? You're not well, are you? The jars are for you, I think. You're running out of time." It was a guess, but even as she said it, she felt it was a good guess. She had glimpsed her own aura in the mirror; it was as shaky as his, but there was more of it. Or maybe it was just brighter, and that's why she thought there was more.

He froze. His eyes got deeper; they withdrew into themselves. Hildy could feel the hostility flare out from him. He relaxed his face a little and tried to be conciliatory. "Well, yes, I imagine my aura is about like yours, a little the worse for wear. I've had my own medical bouts, and I wouldn't mind buying a few jars from you now and then. Mostly now." He gave a little humph at that, a little ironic throat noise.

And then he walked to the window, looked out, turned around, and said, "I'll give you a day to think about it. Don't worry about me," he said, although she wasn't worried. "I'm looking out for you. Some of the others are not as nice as I am." He walked to the door.

"The others? There are others who want to buy my bottles?"

"Some of them will just take your bottles. Not everyone is nice. I know the Bedazzler is on your trail. Don't have anything to do with her."

And he left.

She walked over to the window, watching him cross the street and pass a woman on the corner. They nodded to each other, and then the woman also left.

Once, lying in bed with Noah, she had asked if he would leave his wife for her. He had frowned. "She needs me more than you do. So, no."

"But I need you!" Her heart had plummeted. She had promised herself never to ask the question, and yet it had leapt out of her mouth like a lizard.

He smiled and relaxed. His hair was like a halo.

"No, you *want* me. If I thought you needed me, I wouldn't come back. It would be impossible, satisfying two women's needs. What we have is special and wonderful and free. It's the freedom that keeps me coming back. We choose each other, over and over. Isn't that better than need?"

She had thought about that for months and months. She'd been battling impermanence all her life. Her affair with Noah was punctuated by the shadow of the end, even at the beginning, even in the middle. Had that been a lure for her? Had she found it made Noah more exotic, more lavish? If Noah had been free—she frowned. Her image of Noah immediately became less electric. If Noah had been free, what? Would she have left him? Was she determined to mark any relationship by the loss of the relationship? The minutes drove by, everything of course heading to its end; was that what she had done—created a relationship that always ended (he always went home) and always began again (he came back)? She was the impermanence, not him.

Perhaps it was a result of Michael P's reference to the Bedazzler, but Hildy now often felt she was being followed as she sampled time, being watched; she thought she saw the edges of people moving back from windows, disappearing into doorways. Her own long legs with the red-heeled boots hurried up, trying to catch a better glimpse. She was sure it was a woman; she was sure it was the Bedazzler.

A few days later as she sat in a café, a woman slid into the seat opposite her. She had full hair, streaked white on top of brown, falling to her shoulders. She wore cat-eyed glasses with sparkles on the rim; she had dangling bracelets that glittered as they moved. "Do you mind if I join you?" she asked, though it didn't sound much like a question. She smiled, but it was merely muscles moving; there was nothing relaxed or inviting about that smile.

Her fingers were thin and crowded with rings that also sparkled. There was a powder with glitter that had been applied across her cheekbones. She was in her fifties, Hildy guessed; not far from her own age.

"I'd like to make an offer," she said. "It's not the same offer as Michael P's; I don't want to buy or sell time. But I'm looking for someone, and I've lost the trail. I need you to sample time from certain persons, try to find the time that tells me what I need to know."

Hildy snapped to attention. She was interested in spite of herself. She was being asked to help. And what she was asking for was memories, not time. That didn't seem so problematic. "A detective," she said, interested. "It might be fun. But who are these people? What did they take? Do I want to experience their memories? Wouldn't it be bad?" She saw herself sifting through people's memories, their experiences, finding out the lost bits and perhaps restoring them to the rightful owner. It was startling and innovative. A whole new world opened before her, filled with discoveries. It occurred to her that her ability might help her find out certain things about Noah. Whether he'd been true to her, what his love was really like. Could she solve mysteries like that? Could she really learn to be that adept, that selective? It was dizzying.

"They took my child," the Bedazzler said and leaned back against her seat and stared at Hildy, who felt a little trapped. How could she refuse to help find a child?

"Who did?" Hildy whispered.

"Michael P, or one of his associates. He's always doing dirty work for other people, but it doesn't matter in the end who did it; what matters is getting her back again." She reached into her bag, a loose canvas bag with pink fake gems on it; she brought out a photo of a toddler in a tiara. "That's her," she said. "That's Molly. She's been gone for two months now; stolen out of her bed one night. And I know it was Michael P; he has a habit of leaving his fingerprints around."

"What?" Hildy frowned.

"He leaves fingerprints at various crime scenes; that's what he gets hired for. They give him material someone innocent has handled and he takes their fingerprints and puts them at the crime scene. I don't know how many people he's sent to jail. Innocent people. You have to be careful around him."

"Then why would he leave his own fingerprints?"

"To throw me off." She shrugged. "Of course I'd know it was him. And of course I won't go to the police—"

"Why not?"

"I don't have a good relationship with them," she said. She glared at Hildy, as if it was Hildy's fault. "And I have to keep a low profile, anyway. He's left my fingerprints at various scenes; I don't want the police checking into me at all."

Hildy felt ridiculously unprepared for all of this. A missing child, stolen fingerprints: how was she to judge whether the Bedazzler was any more honest than Michael P? She had stumbled into a world where she was at a loss for the guideposts. "I don't know," she said tentatively. "I don't think I can help you. I'm a little lost, myself. I'm trying to figure out what's happening to me." She tried to sound a little stupid. She looked at the Bedazzler with her eyes open wide.

It was hard to play the ingénue at 49, however.

The Bedazzler smirked. "No good," she said, leaning forward. She put one jeweled hand on top of Hildy's hands. The cut stones caught Hildy's attention; she glanced at the little kaleidoscopic flashes of pink and blue and silver and gray; they were pleasant and had none of the confusion caused by the Bedazzler's words. Her companion moved her other hand so that she clasped Hildy's hand completely, one hand on top, one below. She gave a little squeeze and released it. "You shouldn't have to go through this alone. I know someone will be looking for you soon, the kind of man you deserve. I'm sure you can feel it if you think about it." She smiled kindly and then looked sad. "I know you're having a hard time; I can see you're figuring it out as you go. You're wondering why you should believe me. Why shouldn't you? How many people in your life have asked for help locating a lost child? None, right? And you think, how could you help someone find a child when you know nothing about it? That's why it's true," she said, slipping a ring off her index finger and slipping it on again; off and on. Hildy watched, fascinated. "I'll tell you what," the Bedazzler said. "I'll give you a chance to redeem yourself (you're not making a good impression, you know). Just a little test. Take some of Michael P's time." She grinned and sat back, and then, as Hildy sat there stunned, her mind blinking, the Bedazzler jumped up and sauntered out, with no look back.

The Bedazzler's story—true or not—stayed in Hildy's mind. A child stolen from its mother; it roused sympathy; of course it would. She imagined stealthy figures in the night, a hand clapped over a sleeping child's mouth, the terrible moment when the Bedazzler realized what had happened. Awful.

She wondered who the child's father was. Perhaps the Bedazzler had a man at home. It amazed her, sometimes, which women attracted men, and which did not. It wasn't that Hildy had forsworn men, either, now that Noah was gone. Sometimes she harbored hopes for the future, but cancer certainly changed possibilities. Still, on her way home, she began to imagine meeting an intelligent, sympathetic man, someone like Noah, but attached only to her.

It was a pleasant daydream; she didn't judge herself for it. The man she imagined was younger than she was, as Noah had been younger. Age didn't matter to him, and he was handsome in a quirky way. His features were a little off balance: the nose had been broken once and sat slightly askew; the eyebrows didn't exactly match; he had a warm smile. His hair stood away from his face. He was capable and relaxed and laughed at the right things. He said it himself: he went through life nose-first. Ah, she realized. It was Noah. Noah was alive and waiting for her.

Thinking of him filled her with anticipation, until she realized Noah was dead, and she was alone. There was no one like this in her life. She would remember it, feel disappointed, and then go on to think of him, again slipping into those thoughts without noticing it.

He had a habit of lifting his hand and laying it behind her ear, resting it there, then gently stroking the side of her head and her neck. The weight of his hand was mesmerizing; it stilled her. That hand seemed to have a magic or a subtlety; sometimes it was a prelude to sex, but not always; sometimes he would simply find himself near her (in fact, he felt drawn to her, too, as if by invisible threads) and would face her and lift his hand and cup it along the side of her face back to her ear, the edge of his hand falling onto her neck. What was it called, that turn of the chin bone as it rose up to the ear? There must be a name. The edge of his hand, too, that must have a name, right above the outside of the wrist. All these magical parts coming together, warm and fusing.

When she got home, she thought for a moment that he would be there, and her heart slammed. Of course he wouldn't. She wavered, holding the key right at the lock, and then she went in.

But this was strange.

The apartment felt different.

She knew that *he*—Noah—hadn't been there, but someone had. She rushed over to the bottles on the table and found that six of them were missing.

Michael P; she was certain of it. Couldn't he carry any more than six bottles? Had he forgotten to bring a bag or something? She felt a sting of contempt rising; she couldn't respect him at all; what was he thinking? He didn't even attempt to hide his crime; he merely moved the remaining bottles around a little, as if she didn't know exactly what she had on the table.

Noah disappeared from her thoughts.

She looked at her collection again; she was suddenly exhausted. She took up a bottle labeled E-3M. In her system, that meant energy; the 3M meant the male donor was probably around 30. She inhaled deeply, through her mouth and nose.

That infused her with energy and determination. She could still feel herself, but behind it was a sense of restlessness, determination, self-reliance—she was alive with irritation. These people were playing games with her! If there were games, she had to get ahead of them. She intended to win.

She spent the next hour relabeling her bottles, creating a new system. She put some of them together and labeled them H-2M. What would "H" mean to Michael P? She hoped he would think "health" and be enticed. But these particular jars were gray time.

Her knowledge of auras was growing: she now could identify gray time, those slow late-night hours, as well as sleeping hours; she was learning to identify the different layers by color and movement. She was getting better at scooping out specific areas of color, figuring out how deep they were. Sometimes one color hid behind another, and the time was contradictory, but she was better at it now. Labels with an extra dash meant jars that had some kind of knowledge in them: time spent on electrical wiring, or fixing a car, or picking a lock.

She told herself that she knew the Bedazzler and Michael P were liars and therefore she might not actually be stealing other people's time. Maybe she was just stealing memories. But it *felt* like she was stealing time. She thought of herself as a responsible person. She had done things, of course, which even now made her twinge, but everyone had. She was human. She had followed her own interests, even at the expense of others. But she hadn't pretended that she was innocent. She had accepted her own failures—maybe too readily; maybe too broadly. It was like an exercise routine, developing muscles by repetition, only here she had developed indifference by continuing to do the things she knew she despised, if only to find a way to live.

Because ultimately, she was determined to live.

And until she was absolutely sure she understood how it all worked, she was going to scoop people's auras and record her experiences.

After she changed the labels to the new system, she went out and got more bottles of time—or whatever it was. She was intrigued, whatever it was; she had a strange new skill, and she was going to develop it.

She now carried a large, loose hobo bag, open at the top, and she was swift and silent as she lifted out two jars, opened them, and swept an hour here, an hour there. She chose children skipping home from school or tossing pebbles at a puddle; she chose plumbers and computer programmers (from the looks of them) in case there was something she could learn from them; she avoided bus drivers and cab drivers and store clerks—was this a form of bigotry? And once she plucked time from a doctor who looked exhausted, outside the hospital, grabbing a smoke (she liked the outlawry of it).

She followed men who looked familiar from the back; men whose hands she thought she recognized; but when she caught up with them, they were never the man she imagined. Noah and almost-Noah—it was never him.

Still, she learned what she could from the time she had gathered. She had a few small skills, after a while: she could recall a little French; she could remember how to wire a light switch; she could read Braille, or so she thought; that was harder; certainly her fingers, for a while, kept hovering over objects lightly, trying to figure out what they said.

If she took careful aim when she selected a color in an aura, she could remember a whole scene from someone's life. Once she was a woman riding the subway who saw her ex-lover sitting across from her. They rode together without comment, and she had time to think: what is *he* thinking? He had been hurt, and for a moment or two she had to fight the impulse to go over to him and chat.

The train shook and rattled; the passengers shook gently with it. He didn't come over to *her* and chat. That must mean he didn't want to. It was strange, this sitting across from each other and not acknowledging each other; it almost made her doubt that this was the right man, that this was her ex-lover. Surely he remembered her? But better if he didn't, of course; he had begged her not to leave. Did she look different? Could she believe she had escaped him? Because all the old problems came up: his neediness, his drinking, his impatience—she remembered them, and was right to have ended it.

But how strange, how very strange to sit across the subway from someone you loved once, to sit there and try not to meet his eye (though he wasn't looking her way; he was looking down at his hands). How far emotions wandered. How very sad that was.

All stolen time had stories in it, or at least emotions. Some of them lingered, merging into her own memories. She was pretty sure she could tell the difference between her own and someone else's, though of course once an experience became a memory it took on a character of its own, shuffling into shape as other experiences affected it.

It was time to come up with a plan. Hildy had jars in her closet, in her refrigerator, under her bed. She didn't hear from Michael P for a while. He had finally stolen the jars with gray time in them; he would be quiet until he gave up trying them.

She looked out her window a few days later and saw him across the street, leaning against a wall. She had nothing to worry about with him. She opened her window and waved him up. Better to meet him on her own turf.

"Feeling refreshed?" she asked as she opened the door for him.

"What are you doing? Don't you know I'm on your side?" he asked angrily. He had circles under his eyes; that was what gray time did to you when it released you.

"You stole from me," she said quietly.

"I have to find out what you know." His voice was raspy but a little apologetic. That was new; she wouldn't have put him down for someone who apologized.

"I don't know much. Between you and the Bedazzler, all I can do is guess at what's going on."

"You talked to her," he whispered. "Did she touch you? I told you not to let her touch you."

"No you didn't tell me, and yes she did. So what?"

He leaned toward her, gazing into her eyes. "You think you're in love now, don't you?"

It hit her all at once. Yes, she did. She couldn't stop thinking about Noah, or the person who was almost Noah; she couldn't avoid those daydreams where he touched her neck, or her shoulder, or the small part of her back, sliding his hand up, his chin nuzzling her hair. She could remember him sitting across from her on the subway, smiling at her. No. She knew that was wrong. "What do you mean?" she asked numbly.

"It's what she does." He laughed contemptuously. "She puts all of us in love with some imaginary person. We can never find them; they don't exist; but from now on, your life will be ruled by it."

"No it won't," she said. Her life was already ruled by Noah, wasn't it? "I can handle it."

His shrug involved his head, his shoulders, his back. "That's what I told myself. I used to be with her, and then I left her. But she came up behind me and touched my neck, and I fell in love with her again. I saw her differently, and I went back to her over and over. She touched me each time." He gave a short, scornful laugh. "I would long to see her, and when I saw her I would be disappointed. It was never right between us. I would try to leave, and she would touch me, and I would be sick with wanting her again." He shivered and glared at her. "What did she tell you?"

"You stole her daughter, Molly. She's trying to get her back."

He grimaced. That was becoming his trademark, all these movements and twitches. "She never had a daughter. She wants you to find the meaning."

Had she heard wrong? She reviewed his words for a second, trying to find another word that sounded like it. "Meaning?"

"It's a book," he snapped. "It has all the meaning in the world."

She groaned in exasperation. "None of this makes any sense."

"It's because the meaning is missing," he shouted, sticking his hands out. "She thinks you can find it."

Again, she took time to replay what he'd said and consider it. "Is that what *you* think?"

"I just want the time," he said. "That's all there is to it. It's too late for me to find meaning."

"Oh this is ridiculous. I can't believe in this conversation; it sounds like a comedian's routine."

"Look, we should do this together," he said, holding out his hands palms up. "She's tricky; look what's she's already done to you—made you lovesick and told you lies. I'm straightforward, here; I'll take what I can take but you'll know what it is I'm taking. Time, time, time! That's all I want; quality time and lots of it!"

She had a pang of guilt. His face looked so gaunt; he looked sick and desperate. It made her waver, but what did she know about him, other than that he stole from her and always had a story?

She shook her head. "No. I won't give you anything. I don't know what's going on, and I can't figure out what you really want."

Before she could even think about reacting, he hauled his thin arm back and rammed his fist into her face. She fell down as if all her strings had been cut.

She thought she remembered the sound of glass: bottles jostling each other.

She thought she remembered the door closing.

She floated for a while, her mind drifting as someone ran a hand over her forehead, smoothing her hair. He sat her up tentatively, leaning her against the wall as her head throbbed and her eyes refused to open. She was grateful Noah was there; no matter how awful she felt, it was better to have his strength beside her.

Of course there was no one; Noah no longer existed, except in her mind; she knew it even as she opened her eyes, looking dully around her living room, glancing over to the table where the bottles used to be. The table was empty. Nothing else had been touched as far as she could tell.

She got up slowly, found some aspirin, and gulped down three. She made some coffee and drank it very sweet.

She sat as still as she could, and began to plan.

The next day she set up at one corner of the park, with a small table, rows of large and small jars, two folding chairs, and a sign that said, "Auras read. I can tell you something about yourself. Free."

Mothers wanted to have their children read, and Hildy scrupulously took out a small jar and a large jar, chose the pale-blue part of the aura, and sampled. She'd then take a breath from the small jar, close her eyes, and let a memory come forward. "You have a red truck with a broken door," she might say. "It's your favorite toy." If she got an adult, she'd sample again and report on the pieces of moments she took. "You were once very happy. It felt so good, having him in your life. His name was Gerald." She sampled the pale blues for a while and then tried other colors. Some were not so good, of course; some of them were hours of illness or unhappiness or despair, and she reported them truthfully, and made her notes correlating color and type of memory, until a burly man sat down, smiled at her and said, "I bet you don't really know anything, honey." His "honey" was hostile; it was only pretending to be sexy. She took her jars and sampled a spot that was streaked with dark amber and sat back, stunned.

She could feel her face freeze. Her eyes met her customer's, and they were locked together for minutes, while Hildy's head saw thick hands around a woman's neck, a scream cut off, eyes bulging. She was outside, being herself, being appalled, but she was inside as well, experiencing it, taking satisfaction in it, closing those hands tighter.

The customer noticed something; maybe it was a snap of recognition in her eyes.

"I don't see anything much," she said weakly. "You have a car that was in a crash." She was scrambling for something to say, something that sounded like hokum to the customer, but also had a possibility of truth in it—so it wouldn't seem like she was trying to cover up. "It needed some work on the fender, I think. It's not really clear. Was the car red?" She chose red as an unlikely color for this guy, who no doubt would have a black car, a forgettable car, not wanting to stick out in anyone's mind.

"I have a red car," he said agreeably, surprising her. "A convertible. My kid has it for the weekend. If he puts a scratch on it—" His hand slammed onto the table.

"Okay," she said. "Well, that's all I see. I don't see anyone in it, just that it's sitting by the side of the road, banged up. Maybe a tow truck is coming."

"That kid," he said evenly, his eyes still on her. He was thinking about her, weighing the look she had on her face, no doubt, trying to figure out if she'd recognized him from something—was he wanted?—or not.

She nodded her head and dismissed him, and he wandered a little away from her. She had another customer, an old woman, and she made sure to put a friendly expression on her face after she sniffed the jar (she'd only taken a small jar for the old woman; she had no hours to spare, after all). She told her something from the partial memory she'd gotten, which was luckily about her wedding, some scrap that made the woman smile. Pale blue, with a little streak of green at the edge.

She placed her sign face down soon after that, packing the bottles, making sure that she kept the strangler's jar separate and marked with an X. The jars from the children she put aside in a box of their own; the adults were not very interesting: joggers, store clerks, a plane landing for a vacation in a desert. A mother picking up a carload of small children from soccer practice. All very mundane. Mostly sand-colored.

A man slid in the seat and she smiled. "Well," she said. "Feeling better?"

Michael P frowned. "What do you mean?"

"That knock on the head must have hurt." She made herself sound sympathetic.

"What are you talking about? *You're* the one who got bopped." A look of comprehension hit his face. "Very funny. I didn't do that to you," he said gruffly. "That was the Bedazzler."

"How'd she get in?"

"She has the key. We all have the key. Keys are easy."

Hildy flushed in anger and lifted up her little table and threw it on him. He fell back, his arms flailing, and landed on the ground. Hildy felt a small surge of satisfaction—it felt like the strangler's satisfaction, she thought. She calmed her mind.

A few people stared; one woman who had been approaching swerved off to the side; a child clapped its hands.

"They fall so easily," a woman said behind her, laughing. Hildy recognized the Bedazzler and turned with a scowl.

"You!" Hildy cried. "Did you hit me on the head?"

"It looks like you're the one who goes around whapping people," the Bedazzler said, blinking her eyes lazily.

"Did you? Michael P said you did."

"What else did he say?" The Bedazzler picked up the tray Hildy had hit Michael P with; he was sitting up now, shaking his head; she stepped over him to put the tray back.

"There is no baby," Hildy said. "No Molly."

The Bedazzler frowned; it took up all of her face. Her mouth did a moue, her eyebrows furrowed, her shoulders crept up, her eyes looked at Hildy with disappointment. The glitter on her ceased to glitter; it was as if a shadow stepped over her; she wore a jacket with sequins that didn't glint, a gaucho skirt, and, surprisingly, thong sandals. She looked wonderful, however; Hildy wished she could wear clothes with such confident contempt. Though that hardly mattered. Was Michael P correct in saying that the Bedazzler had broken in and hit her?

"Did you break in to my apartment?" she asked.

The Bedazzler lifted her chin. Her eyes sparkled suddenly, whether it was reflected off her sequins or not, Hildy couldn't tell. "I'd be ashamed of myself if a *key* could keep me out. Would it keep you out? And by key, I mean anything that gets me where I'm not supposed to be."

Hildy thought, suddenly, that she might have done wrong by Michael P. Maybe he was right after all. Clearly, the Bedazzler didn't mind breaking into her apartment. She looked and Michael P was gone, the only evidence he'd been there was a fall of leaflets she'd made up and which he'd dumped when he'd crashed after she hit him.

Poor Michael P. Maybe the Bedazzler was the seriously annoying person, not Michael P. Or maybe they were having fun with Hildy, batting her between them.

"What's this book of meaning?" Hildy asked. She looked away; she was trying to pretend she was jaded, that all these games, after all, were no real interest to her.

But she caught how the Bedazzler stilled herself: the eyes went cautious, the mouth stretched itself tight; her chin froze. Hildy forced herself to consider the ears— were the ears lying when the Bedazzler repeated, "Book of meaning?"

She's heard of it, Hildy thought. "It's obvious you've heard of it."

The Bedazzler frowned and pursed her lips and appeared to be thinking.

"What's this book?" Hildy demanded again. It was better to be bearish, she thought; it was better to play the tough guy than the accommodating one. It wasn't her usual role, but with chemo in her veins maybe her usual role had to change.

The Bedazzler was quiet for a moment; Hildy could see her try out one thought then another. It offended her to watch this. "You might as well tell me the truth," she said. "I can go with Michael P, or I can go with you." She jutted her chin out in irritation, and it felt good to do it. Body language, she thought: you do something with your body, and your mind follows.

"All right," the Bedazzler said and exhaled. Body language there, too. Hildy thought: it looked like she'd given in.

"There's a book; it's true. It holds the meaning to life." She shrugged her shoulders. "See? It's so simple. Michael P talked about it, but he never explained it. A book of meaning." She said it as if exasperated. "Even people like him can be lucky; they can find things they don't deserve. Apparently he found it or read it or had it. But then he lost it. His mind is going," she said casually. "He put it down somewhere and forgot." She arranged her jacket, covered with sparkles, so that it fit her better. "That's where you come in. You have to sample his time until you find that memory, that moment when he put it down. Because it's connected to Molly. I think he had Molly with him."

She leaned close to Hildy, breathing on her. Hildy moved back, away from her. She had already been infected with this longing for a man who might be Noah, or a ghost of Noah; she was afraid the Bedazzler would give her some other longing, now: something even harder.

The Bedazzler straightened up when she noticed it; her eyes were mocking.

"First it's Molly who's gone missing, now it's a book." This was all a little bit suspicious, Hildy thought.

"The book exists," the Bedazzler said. "And it's important. If you find Molly for me, you'll see how important it is."

Hildy took a moment to look at the Bedazzler's ears and her eyes and her face. She was not easy to read, but then Hildy was new to the game. The Bedazzler held her gaze as if she was watching for a way in. So, Hildy thought; she's still withholding something. "Why should I believe you?" she asked, as if idly. A book like that, she thought: a lot of people would hold onto it. If it existed. Michael P said the baby didn't exist. Maybe the book didn't either.

The Bedazzler smiled. "There are secrets in the world," she said gently. "People suddenly see things—like you have suddenly seen things. The book explains that, I think. That's what Michael P said. Who knows if he was right? But whoever took Molly took the book. Or the other way around. I don't know why it isn't clear to me. I know it sounds strange," she said, trying very hard to concentrate on what obviously kept slipping away from her. "It must be shock. But the book does exist. Molly exists. I mean, if someone had told you that you could see time, and steal time—now what would you have thought? And yet," she ended, musing, "and yet you can, and yet you do. Right?" This last question was thrown at her, a challenge. "Would you have believed it?"

Hildy considered all of it. Of course she would never have believed it, but now there was no choice. What did it mean, to be forced to believe something unbelievable? What did it change, to become the something unbelievable yourself?

"But what do you want me to do?"

"Find them. Find both of them," the Bedazzler hissed, and she was gone.

More than a year earlier, Noah had failed to keep his appointment with her and had failed to call. Hildy was allowed to call him at the office, but not at home. No texts, no emails either. He didn't want a trail. He was reliable, he said, like a big old dog. He would never just disappear.

They had arranged to meet on a Friday nigh ("working late," as he often told his wife). Hildy waited and waited, going over her last conversation with him. "I'll see you Friday at six or so. We'll go to the park and watch couples making out in the bushes." He had laughed, that thrilling laugh of his. The hours came and went. This wasn't good; it couldn't be good. Would he end it without telling her? No, of course not. He had sworn he wouldn't do that. All the rules were in place to protect his wife; maybe something had happened to her. But he would have gotten in touch. He was a man who showed respect.

She would call him on Monday. She would hear his voice and his explanation. Of course she'd known all along that something like this would happen. She was angry with herself for being in this position. Why hadn't she prepared herself for it? That was the weekend she painted her boot heels red. It was dramatic. She felt dramatic.

The day after the Bedazzler told her about the Book of Meaning, Hildy saw the man who was Noah or almost-Noah. He walked past her on the street as she left after her next chemo, wobbly and buzzing with drugs. She stumbled after him, spitting once as a small ripple of nausea hit her. He got farther ahead of her because of it, but she was only able to keep him in sight until he turned a corner, and when she reached it, he was gone. Instead, Michael P was there, leaning against a building, as if waiting to meet her.

"Are the colors brighter today?" he whispered. She was forced to lean against the building next to him, to catch her breath. She squinted at the people passing by, and she could see the swirls of time; indeed they were brighter. She blinked, hoping to clear them away.

"They are," she sighed.

"There's money in it," he reminded her. "And now you can see which hours to take more accurately, can't you?

You have to get the best hours of all; you have to figure it out. I'll pay you for the best hours, whatever you want."

His hours were thin and ragged. "You want them for yourself," she said. "You're not selling them to anyone else."

"I need them," he admitted. "If you keep at it, you'll need them too. But you don't need them now, not yet. So in the meantime...." He jerked himself upright. "I'll give you a day to get some more."

"I'll need more than a day," she said faintly. "I'll be sick all day tomorrow. Maybe after that."

He seemed to relax a little, hearing that. "All right. The day after tomorrow. Don't fail me," he said, gripping her elbow. "I can be unpleasant. I need more time!"

He nodded abruptly, as if they'd made an agreement. She watched him as he made his way across the street, his body seeming even more knobby and disordered.

She put on her jacket two mornings later, deciding she would go out for a cup of coffee and a brioche. She loved the word *brioche*, and she was beginning to get her appetite back. She stuck her hand into her jacket pocket and felt a business card. Odd; she didn't remember putting one in there. The card read only *Swami Ben* and an address.

She put the card down, determined to ignore it, but she didn't throw it away. She realized that meant she might use it, so she did throw it away. Then she thought she might need it, so she got it out of the garbage. Who had put the card in her pocket?

If she ignored it, then she would be giving it too much importance. Or was that just a trick to convince herself that it wasn't important? She got tired of it, the spirals in her brain. She would go to the address on the card after she had her brioche just to see, just to get rid of it.

The address was a very small storefront in a semi-industrial part of the city. What kind of foot traffic would anyone get here? There were no curtains, no signs, nothing to break the emptiness of the window. And inside the window, a man in a short-sleeved checked shirt sat on a wooden bench, leaning against a piano and just looking out at the street. He caught her eye and motioned her in. Hildy sighed to herself—just a little note of resignation—and went in.

"You're Swami Ben?" she asked.

"I was expecting you." He looked delighted as he rushed toward her; he had a huge grin and flung his arms wide, as if to hug her. She stood still; it was unusual for perfect strangers to be so happy to see her, and she was immediately suspicious.

"Expecting me?" she asked, her voice a little sharp. She meant it to be sharp.

He stopped, dropped his arms, and tilted his head a little. "I am so sorry," he said. "I know about you, and you don't know about me. You're here because I have information for you."

"Which is?"

He was a few inches shorter than she was, and he was a little too stout for his clothes. His buttons pulled. What kind of swami eats too much? she wondered.

"I understand you have a talent," he said, motioning her to a folding chair with a ripped naugahyde seat; she sat on it and watched as he sat back on his bench and folded his hands together. She thought, resignedly, that of course he could see she had no hair and was going through chemo; she was easy to recognize. He had been told about her. "Talent," he repeated. "Talent is a wonderful thing, once you know how to use it. Wouldn't you agree?"

He waited for her reply, so she nodded unenthusiastically.

"What talent is that?" she asked. She was in some kind of game, as far as she could tell, but she wasn't going to give in so easily. Let him tell her what he knew; she wasn't offering anything.

"Why, you can see time!" he cried. He was delighted. His eyebrows rose up; he lifted himself slightly from the bench; his voice squeaked with excitement.

Weren't swamis supposed to be more restrained? "How do you know?" she asked.

"Why, just about everyone *knows*," he chortled. "You're not very good at keeping secrets. You tell everyone, in one way or another. Anyone who might be interested — I don't necessarily mean you tell the people you *steal* from; you don't do that, do you?" His mouth hung open a little, he leaned forward and waited for her answer.

"You don't," he said, nodding and sitting back. "People with gifts are like that; they give and they take without much interest in the morality of it. Don't you agree?"

It was a leading question, and she wouldn't answer it. Morality was something she would think about soon, when anything at all became clear. Or maybe not. She had cancer; what did morality have to do with anything once you have cancer?

"Who told you about me?" she asked.

"Why, everyone knows about you!" he repeated, surprised.

That made her queasy; she swallowed and breathed in. "Who put your card in my pocket?"

"A number of people could have done that—the baldies, the Bedazzler, Michael P, many alternative medicine practitioners, why there's hundreds of people, really. We all know each other, and now we know you!" His voluminous grin popped up again; it was an endearing grin, there was no denying it.

Baldies? She would think about that later. She controlled her breathing. "Why? Why do they want me to meet you?"

"I can help you find Molly." He looked at her expectantly.

She closed her eyes briefly, then opened them to glare at him. "There is no Molly."

His head jerked back; his eyes flared open. "Really? But I know her. I've known her for years."

"For years? I thought she was a child, a toddler, a baby—something very young." Hildy felt a slight dizziness, a fatigued dizziness, spilling around her vision. She had no desire to figure any of this out; she wanted someone else to make it clear.

"You said there is no Molly, but you thought she was a baby? Isn't that contradictory?"

"Oh, please," Hildy snapped wearily; her head was really starting to pound. "Let's stop the games. Is there a Molly? Is she the Bedazzler's child? Where is she, and what does it matter to me?"

The swami leaned over and took her hands. His fingers were cool and much longer than Hildy would have thought; she could feel them as if they were a tall, thin man's fingers, not wrapped in fat; they were gentle but firm, and she felt more relaxed while he held on to her. There was nothing wrong with being more relaxed, so she stilled herself for a few minutes and simply let him hold her hands. The tension released itself in her head. "That's better," she said, nodding. "Thank you. You have some kind of healing effect."

He laughed. "I'm dedicated to the spiritual arts. I can relieve stress; I can tell you how to live a good life. It's a profession, after all, and I'm good at it."

"All right, I'll bite. How can I live a good life?"

"Find Molly," he said firmly.

"I've been told to look for the book of meaning instead."

"Molly has it. Michael P gave it to her years ago, before he was ill. He told her to keep it safe, and then he forgot it all."

She shook her head. "Then tell me how to find her."

"I don't know; but Michael P once did. You have to find out from him."

Her mouth got tight; she glared at the swami, who laughed. "You have to sample his time. You have to sample his past. You have to find the time he doesn't remember, and that's how you'll find whatever you need to know."

He nodded at her brightly, got up, and sat behind his piano. "I also give piano lessons, by the way. My student will be here shortly. Sorry."

"But you haven't told me how to do that!"

"Oh?" He ran a trill of chords. "Well, you have noticed that forgotten memories have a little dark swirl in them?"

"No, I haven't noticed that. How do you know?"

"Michael P told me a long time ago," he said, as the door cracked open and a man leaned in, saying, "Am I early?"

"No, you're not early," the swami said.

"So good to see you again," the visitor commented to Hildy. "It's been a while. You should come set up another appointment with me." He nodded and paused, waiting for Hildy to leave.

I know him? Hildy wondered, and then it clicked for her: the acupuncturist!

"But how would Michael P know?" she asked, turning to the swami, trying to gather her wits as she stood and headed for the door.

"He's one of you," the swami said. "Or at least, he *was.*"

As she left, looking back from the sidewalk to where the acupuncturist was beginning his lesson, she could hear the fumbling strains of "Sweet Adeline."

A song she'd never liked. The universe was a strange and heavy place.

⟍

When she got home, she organized her bottles while sipping her herbal tea. She had occasionally noticed gradations in the colors she saw, but she hadn't known what they meant. It was time to find out.

The next morning, she ran her hands over her bald head; she penciled in some eyebrows; she dressed and put on her clothes and her kick-ass boots. Her backpack held all sorts of bottles; she was going to continue sampling, testing out her theories about what the different colors and combinations meant, since after every chemo she saw them more clearly than before. She walked the streets, staring at people—not really *at* them; around them. Some pedestrians glanced at her, annoyed, only to notice that her eyes weren't on *them*, but somewhere around them. She saw depth, and gradations, and small pieces of movement in some areas, and some stillness in others. She knew the grayness of gray time, but there were bright splashes of colors that reflected bright times until the brightness began to burn into the retina; she thought these might be times of terrible realizations and failures, and that the greens were the beginnings of things, and the blues and purples—were they memories of dreams or hopes: she would have to find out.

It troubled her that the swami had said to sample Michael P's time; he clearly had so little left, and she could accidentally take some of the unused time. She wasn't sure how to exclude it.

She wanted to find out how to tell the lost memories from the remembered ones, and how to tell recent ones from old ones.

She sighed: it was interesting; it was difficult. Only a woman with a cancer of the tempora and boots with red kitten heels could do it.

She went to Central Park and opened a notebook and penciled in some thoughts; she wanted to look like a writer struggling with inspiration. She could stare moodily without attracting attention.

Yes, all right; she could see, in some of the colors, a very small swirl; it was difficult because there were so many colors next to and behind; but yes, she thought she could discriminate which blocks had the sign in them. She stood up and walked around and took a few.

But what would that do? How could she tell if these were memories that people had forgotten? She stood in line for a pretzel, and took something from the person in front of her; she dropped her notebook and took a sampling from the man who bent to pick it up; but what would she learn from that?

She finally gave it up for the moment. It seemed to her that the only real way of testing this was to sample her own time. That would be the only way she'd hit on a forgotten bit of time. She hadn't wanted to do that; it seemed confusing to sample her own aura. But what else could she do?

Deep in thought, she suddenly came across a gathering of bald people in the park. It was a sunny day; perhaps that's why the women had taken off their scarves and hats and wigs; all together, men and women, they looked like the meeting of a sect of some kind; a sect of bald ones. For a brief moment, she considered taking off her own scarf, but didn't. The nape of her neck always felt chilled now; it made her wonder how bald men handled it, being so unprotected. She was wearing a woven Guatemalan belt around her own head scarf; it was meant to look like a fashion, though she'd never been particularly in step with fashion.

The bald ones eyed her as she approached. A young woman came toward her, asking, "Are you new here?" She wore jeans and a sweatshirt and good shoes.

"I'm new here, yes," Hildy said guardedly. "Is this a meeting? A support group?"

The young woman snorted. "Support group? Okay. That's good. We're all in the same boat, anyway." She looked at Hildy's scarf. "What kind of cancer?"

Hildy put her hand up to her scarf self-consciously. "Brain. Specifically, tempora cancer."

"Temporal lobe?"

"No. That's what everyone thinks, but it's the tempora, the part that keeps track of time."

The woman let out a huge sigh. "I've heard of it." She turned back to the other baldies. "She's the one," she yelled back to the crowd, who were all watching closely. As one, they surged and surrounded Hildy. It was terribly alarming. Too quickly, she discovered that there was no way to get away from them, short of fighting her way out. She thought it must be some kind of assault, some kind of gang thing. Why not? There were all kinds of gangs, why not cancer gangs? She swung her backpack off her back and clutched it to her chest.

"We're not going to hurt you," the woman said, surprised by Hildy's movements. "We need your help; we all do. We're the ones who won't make it. I'm Grace. Cervical." She looked to her right. "This is Babe, and Will, and Antoinette. Breast, leukemia, bone. And Rob, John, Phil. Liver, skin, and brain (not your kind of brain). We're all metas, metastatic. We've been going through all the drugs, but it's spread for all of us. You can get us time," she said quickly. "Let's cut to the chase. We're all running out of time and you can get it. We know you can. Michael P told us. He said there was someone. It's you, right?" Her voice rose at the end, rose with hope and not a little anger. She was leaning into Hildy's space; she was claiming it.

Hildy's eyes looked over the crowd, noting faces that seemed healthy, even plump, and others that were haggard and grim. Their eyes were locked on her. One of them—Rob?—was moving his lips, and she paused until she could figure out what he was saying: "I'm dying." That was all. Her eyes noted the aura around him, weak and almost shivering. Lowering her head, she loosened the grip on her backpack. "I guess I'm the one," she said. "Michael P is always stealing time from me. But I'm still learning how to choose which hours are best. I make mistakes. He's gotten gray time from me more than once."

"Gray time," Rob murmured. "I'd take that. I could be comfortable knowing that I had an extra hour to live, even if I only stared at the walls during it. You can stare during gray time; that's what I do, mostly, anyway. Stare and think about what's coming next. Gray time? I'll take it."

The others, too, began to say they'd take any kind of time at this point—anything she could find for them, troubled time (what was that, Hildy wondered), down time, mean time, vacation time—they began to make fun of the whole concept—first time, not the last time of course, springtime, summertime. They weren't proud and they could pay! They'd pay in any way Hildy wanted. If she wanted money, they had money; if she needed anything done, they had family who could get it done. "Suppertime!" someone yelled belatedly, and they all laughed. They were relieved and maybe even buoyant. Hildy caught it, and laughed as well.

She felt for them. She could feel them all relaxing, and she did too, recognizing how they were all connected. She knew what it felt like when the needle entered her skin and the first rush of the chemo—always chilled, always chilling her—flushed through her veins. They knew, too; they'd felt it more often than she had, been through it again and again. They knew the taste in the mouth, the sores, the nausea, the dread, the determination to fight. Her battle was still early; their battle was late. Two different stages of time. They'd heard regret in their doctors' voices again and again, and they had still felt hope for a new treatment, and then learned that it had failed, again.

She swung her backpack to the ground and knelt down as she opened it and showed them her bottles. "I haven't recorded all these yet, but they come from young people. I still have to make sure, but I think I can give you a good guess." She took out her chart. "Childhood. School. Getting caught in a lie. Losing a pet. Getting a new pet. First day on a new job." She held them out, one by one, and someone took it each time. "Dessert, I think. Or at least a sweet is involved, maybe even birthday cake. This one, I think, is something shameful." A hand withdrew. "I'll keep it. But here again, something very young, a toy, a bike, I'm not sure," and it was grabbed immediately. "I've got some that I'm thinking might be about love; I'm not sure. A very pale blue. The darker blues are not as nice. There are some educational ones, always bright orange. Religion, usually in the deep purples. I don't have all the nuances; the colors mix up a little, but this is cherry red, it seems cheerful to me." She closed her bag. "The little bottles are only minutes long, they're what I use to test and classify." She sat back on her heels and looked at them.

"What do you want?" Grace said politely, clutching her bottle. "In exchange?"

What did she want? Hildy closed her eyes briefly. There were so many things she wanted to know. She opened her eyes. "Can you get me some information? I don't trust Michael P. And I need to know more about the Bedazzler. Find out who she is; find out what she's after."

She could feel how alert everyone got as soon as she mentioned the Bedazzler. As if she'd said something wrong. How could she have said anything wrong? She didn't know enough to be right or wrong.

Grace finally broke the tension. "All we know is that she watches Michael P. She always shows up when he comes here."

Hildy's head shot up. "He comes here? He's part of your group? He…." She trailed off, not sure how to ask the question. Her eyes roamed unhappily around the group, with their bald heads, their greedy eyes.

"Of course he comes here," Grace said, surprised. "He's one of us." She hesitated only for a second. "He's dying."

꡷

Hildy took what remained of her jars home. They were the small samples, but she'd noted the color and the body location of each in her notebook.

She set up a big color wheel poster she'd gotten from an art store. She had colored pins as well, and she moved back and forth between the poster and her index cards and notebook, trying to identify each bit of time according to feeling, sensation, a guess at the perceived age of the person at the time of the memory because a memory of being grabbed by the arm at three is different from a memory of being grabbed at fifty. That background sense of one's age increased with time: the young never think about it except when it's a handicap to be young, but the old feel it behind every sensation. She had a poster of the human body next to the color chart, and here she began to cross-reference the donor's age and the depth of color, to try to see if she could get more precise in pinpointing the way colors changed with time. But she needed a three-dimensional human body to work with, because colors arrayed themselves on all sides.

She went online and ordered a plastic full-length skeleton. When it came, she hung it on the stand it came with, but the skeleton, with its unflinching sockets and disapproving jaw, was too stark. She dressed it in jeans and a tee-shirt; she bought a cheap mask from a costume store and painted it pale pink to give it life, and put a dot of darker pink on the cheekbones. She added boots. She gave it a cap.

She constructed a wire dome and hung it from the ceiling, and put the skeleton doll under it. She hung fishing line from the dome all the way down to the floor — rows and rows of line, so she could identify distance from the body to the edge of the aura. She needed to begin using her references to create a map around the body, as she learned more and more.

For a few days after meeting the baldies, Michael P and the Bedazzler left her alone, as far as she could tell. She looked out her window frequently, but she didn't see Michael P's hunched figure across the street, watching for her. She changed her locks and set up a camera on her computer. And in case the Bedazzler stole the computer, she had it on automatic backup.

Hildy surveyed her apartment: the jars, the records, the posters, the doll with its made-up aura. She felt efficient.

She sat down, suddenly tired. Of course she was tired. She was going through chemo. All at once, despair. The baldies—she didn't want to be around them. They were a bad version of her future. She wouldn't go back; that was definite. How could she help them, really? She would never be able to get enough bottles for all of them all the time. And she might need the bottles herself, someday. Though if Michael P kept breaking in and stealing them, what chance did she have?

Fatigue spread through her. She didn't want to help anyone else; she wanted to concentrate on herself. She was in a battle; did she have to save them as well? Was it fair?

She lay down on her couch, closing her eyes for a moment. She should get up and make something healthy to eat: she had started reading up on diets for cancer, on vitamins and minerals and which greens held the best nutrition. She had gone macrobiotic for a week; then she had decided that she needed comfort food, and comfort food wasn't macrobiotic. She was crawling her way through treatment, wishing for the best outcome. She had practiced positive thinking; she had envisioned herself fighting the cancer cells; she had gone along with it all patiently. But maybe anger was the right response? Maybe her cancer cells were feeling coddled and sympathized with instead of feeling threatened?

Was she strong enough? That was what she wanted to know: could she win this fight? She thought of the baldies again. She hadn't gotten to know them, their personalities or their struggles, but surely they were the ones who had fought hard, or they would be home wrapped up in blankets and sipping herb teas? She should help them; they deserved it.

She should start a special collection box where she could keep the best time she found, for herself. The other bottles could go to them—if they wanted them, the lesser hours, why not?

She fell asleep facing the hanging time-doll and dreamt that she had a warehouse full of hours, correctly labeled, enough hours for a lifetime, maybe two. She would not die.

The next day she decided to test herself.

She sat in front of a full-length mirror, with the doll hanging behind her as a kind of template. She knew by now that no two people matched up exactly, since their experiences were different, but there were areas that lined up generally. The left was emotional, the right was time rooted in physical action, though these were rough demarcations. Older memories were lower; recent ones were higher; but again, these were just guides. There were threads of colors that wove up and down—physical actions or emotions that had echoes through time or that fed into earlier themes. No bit of time was completely disconnected.

What of her own time? What did she want to sample? She was still haunted by Noah and the almost-Noah and didn't feel up to testing her recent past. But if she stayed to the time on her right side, found a forgotten memory there, it would most likely (if her theories were correct) be associated with an event that involved action. And if she stayed with the cheery tones on the lower edge, then it would be a happy time from childhood.

Hildy opened a bottle and studied the mirror, looking for an early time with a gradation in it, and scooped. She capped it quickly, then marked it with its location and its colors.

She wondered if people felt differently when their time was taken. Did she feel different?

She opened the jar and inhaled.

Of course how much did anyone remember of childhood? The traumas, yes, but the everyday? She had gotten a skateboard when she was eight or so; it was for her birthday. The next-door neighbor's child was having a party, a graduation party from grammar school. This was before every child had a party every year; when she was young, parties were rare. She didn't get one for her birthday but she was wearing a birthday corsage (it was made of dog biscuits; she had nibbled on one) while she watched her neighbor's party.

The skateboard topped the other gifts, of a blouse and a Bobbsey Twins book. She was allowed to go to the park, where there was a hill with a concrete path. She rode it down slowly the first time, then faster and faster. The vibrations from the pavement rode up her legs; if she closed her mouth, her teeth rattled; so she closed her mouth. She thought she was going very fast. Enormously fast.

She ran into a crack in the pavement and sailed off into the air, landing on a grassy area. The moment when she sailed into the air was blissful. It was surprising, and it had no thoughts in it; it was pure sensation. The landing also knocked any thoughts out of her head. She lay there, her breath knocked out.

She sat up; she had a scrape on her elbow.

She took the skateboard up the hill and aimed it for the crack again.

What did that say about her, that she would deliberately try to crash again? Was it a good characteristic? Was it a childish version of a death-wish? No; it illustrated a desire for sensation. Had that been true for the rest of her life? She lost herself in that thought. Her loves, her work; what had happened to that little girl? She was having trouble tracing her through the rest of her life.

But was that little girl right, anyway? She could have seriously hurt herself, though Hildy didn't remember that happening. Perhaps she hadn't hit the sweet spot again; she certainly didn't remember breaking any bones.

And then she remembered that she had sipped her own time, and she jolted upright again, blinking, looking around the room. She looked at the clock to see how long a sample she'd taken, but was annoyed that she hadn't noted the time when she began. It was always slipping away, wasn't it?

And that had been a forgotten memory; she was fairly sure. Although now that it was a recovered memory, it was hard to be absolutely certain. It had been sweet, though, having all her history ahead of her, sailing through the air, flying, free.

When did the past start? Was it a second ago, a minute ago?

It struck her that she couldn't be sure that what she was thinking was happening in the present. Was this what she was thinking now or memories of earlier thoughts?

Was she even sure this was the present? How did she know that she wasn't just living something she'd drunk from a bottle? This was the present, wasn't it?

Stop it, she told herself. Let it go, she insisted. How, indeed, could she tell what the present was anymore? It all seemed to be happening right then, right there, even when she was living through someone else's hours. But she knew the difference, didn't she? No matter what, she could always tell when she was herself again, herself in the present, with her own thoughts and her own memories. She caught sight of her hand, with an empty bottle in it, and put the bottle down.

Noah's secretary Carla, didn't answer when Hildy rang his office. She hesitated, asking after Carla, being told she had taken the day off. "Well, actually, I was looking for Noah. I'm a friend of his," she finally said.

There was a silence at the other end, and Hildy's heart began to pound.

"I'm so sorry," the stranger said. "Noah died on Thursday. They think it was an aneurism. On the subway. They stopped the train, but by the time the EMTs got there, it was too late. Are you all right?"

A single sob sailed out of Hildy. She held herself rigid. "The funeral?"

"It was this morning. I can give you the charity his family chose instead of flowers." Hildy was silent. "Do you want to send a card? Do you want the address?"

"I have the address," Hildy said. "I've always had the address."

Isn't it odd, she thought: all the minutes of our lives hidden in our auras, hidden in our heads, including the day I heard of Noah's death. What color would that day be, she wondered idly. And how much of that color did she have? Her time with Noah was fragmented, by necessity. If she put it all together, if she could count all the time they had together, could see it arrayed like a scarf around her head—how much time would that be?

He had parceled it out, and she had agreed to it. But his wife—Eileen—possessed waves of time with him, memories surrounding her like a wedding veil, sprayed out, mobile. After his death, Hildy had concentrated on just going on living. She had set out to survive, and she had. She had endured sorrow like perpetual bad weather. Someday it would lift, she'd told herself. Someday she would be beyond sorrow. Of course she knew that wasn't totally true. You never completely release sorrow; it's stored, all the pieces of it. There may be some small memories of Noah I've forgotten, she thought. But every memory of him is important. I don't want to forget anything about him. But it had already happened, she knew. She had forgotten things and would forget more.

What's the point of having all these memories, then? At the end of my life, carrying memories that I can't possibly remember or access anymore: what's the point? Wouldn't it be easier just to keep the ones that matter? Some sort of physical law could get rid of remembering visits to the dentist and the gynecologist, the weekly math test in the fourth grade, waiting for a stop light on my way to the store—all of them kept somewhere for no good reason.

She had no answers.

Was it just the nature of time to be like a flood, just an indiscriminate wall of water carrying everything with it? All that rushing and carrying, just to get to the end? There was no other purpose for a flood, for memories: just to get to the end, just to move, just to go forward to the end, the end, the end.

It was putting her in a very bad mood, all these thoughts of time, all this hunger for it, when all she could do was stall it for a little while, until it was all gone.

⚊

"I looked up that side effect you told me about—the auras you said you saw?" Anne, the chemo nurse, smiled at her; she was always supportive and warm. This was a profession that made a difference, Hildy thought: she was a god, this woman, a giver of life and hope and renewal.

"I don't remember telling you," she said.

"Keeping secrets, are you?" Anne asked gaily. "Don't. You and I, we're in this together, so don't exclude me."

"I won't," Hildy promised weakly. She was going through her mind, searching for the memory of telling Anne; she thought she found it, finally, and wondered what color it was. "And what did they say about it?"

"Oh, it's been reported a few times. No warnings associated with it, which means no bad outcomes in people who reported them. So I think you're safe." She grinned. "Still seeing them?"

"Yes. Stronger each time."

"Are they useful? I mean, can you tell anything from them?"

"I'm still trying to figure that out. There's no decoder ring, if that's what you mean. The trick is to figure out what each color means and then each shade within it."

"Sounds like a lot of work. Benadryl first; what kind of ice pop do you want?" She hung a bag of Benadryl off the rack; on the other hook on the rack were the other two bags of chemo; one of which caused sores in the mouth that could be helped if the patient sucked on ice pops.

"Orange?" Orange was the color of learning, of surprises; she could use that.

Anne handed Hildy a blanket, which she wrapped around herself. The drugs were so cold, and then the ice pop—it was chills and more chills for the next two hours.

"My cancer is rare," Hildy said as Anne finished up.

"Yes, it is," Anne said .

"Have you ever known another person who had it?"

"Ah," Anne said. "I see. Well, it's surprising, but I have known another tempora cancer. A man. Five or six years ago, I think. Haven't seen him since, but that doesn't mean much. He could be cured; he could have switched doctors."

"Was his name Michael?" Hildy asked.

Anne cocked her head a little, going through her mind. Hildy watched closely. There was a little eddy, almost a small pulse, in the creamy yellow area next to Anne's shoulder. She made a note to test that area. Memories of work? Memories of work that year? And how interesting to see that if you asked a person to recall something, that area moved. Make a note of it.

"Michael," Anne agreed, a little surprised. Hildy could see that same area calm down; that area held Michael in Anne's mind, she was sure. "Do you know him?"

"I've met him. He's not doing well."

"Sorry. It doesn't mean you won't."

Hildy lifted her chin. "I really wasn't talking about me," she said, surprised. And then she had to ask herself, No? Didn't every other person with cancer get sorted out: worse than me, better off than me, had a bad attitude, had a bad doctor. Everything she heard came back to herself. She winced. "Sorry. That's not true. I do wonder what went wrong with him."

"He was more advanced," Anne said. "And I think he dropped out of treatment after a while—or did he go to an alternative treatment? Holistic was getting a lot of press a few years back. I seem to remember waiting for him, and then he didn't show up. I called, and his wife said she was sure he'd rescheduled. I could be wrong," Anne trailed off.

"His wife?" The chills were already hitting Hildy; she pulled the blanket close around her shoulders; she took a second blanket from Anne and laid it over her lap. Anne began to infuse the second bag, the red bag, the horrible bag of drugs. Not that Hildy could really tell the difference in effects between the first and second chemo bags; maybe it was the color red that did it. In auras, red meant extremes of some kind—extreme fear, danger, love, pain; extreme loss. So it is with chemo, Hildy thought: your cure must first destroy you. The way to life is through death.

"Well," Anne said. "I've seen a lot of patients. I could be mixing him up with someone else. I'm pretty sure he didn't tell her at first, because when I asked if anyone was coming to pick him up after the first chemo, he said no one, and I asked, where was his wife? Some people don't tell; some people feel ashamed; some people can't stand pity. There's a whole host of reasons for the way people act, and they don't have to make sense to me. Me, I would organize my own funeral. And I like having people around me. But Michael—well, who knows, really? They should do a study on personality traits and prognosis; it may have more to say than stages of cancer. That's what I think."

Hildy loved the soothing sound of Anne's voice, the certainty of Anne's viewpoints. To Anne, life was a series of accomplishments. You simply had to figure out how to get there; what to say, what to do. She had been a chemo nurse for seven years; she admitted that she hadn't quite figured out her approach in the beginning. Now she felt she was in sync with the patients; she was fighting along with them; she was willing to listen without any caveats; she had learned to be sympathetic above all else. When her patients cried, she let them; she didn't bully them into bravery; she cheered them into it. When they were fearful, she sat with them and told them stories about patients who had lived 20, 30, 50 years past chemo; she figured out what she needed to say, and she said it. Even the difficult patients really wanted to believe they would live; they wanted to be coached into having that belief again. If they believed that, then chemo was a snap. If they didn't believe, then they fell apart under chemo. The trick was to find what would make them believe.

"He has a mustache," Hildy said, trying to get Anne to go back to Michael. "Thick dark hair and a mustache. A little taller than me, thin. A way of standing a little too close?" The mustache was fake, she knew; but who would wear a fake mustache except a cancer patient who missed his real mustache? Of course his hair should have grown back by then. She wouldn't be at all surprised to learn Michael P shaved off his mustache every day, and put a fake one on.

"Hmm," Anne said. "That sounds right. That sounds like him. But as I said, I see a lot of people. I wouldn't swear that I've got it right. I found him a little tricky, that's all. I was worried when he skipped out on treatment. He was the first, for me, the first who quit. That always makes you feel like you should have done more. Though now I know—" she tapped the bag and looked over across the room to another woman on another bag of chemo—"now I know it has nothing to do with me at all."

She walked away with a wave and began to check that other woman's bag (which wasn't red chemo, Hildy noted: what did *she* have?).

What if Michael P and the Bedazzler were indeed married? Her forehead began to contract; it was a lot of concentration, given the circumstances. Did she care if they were married? Did it make anything clearer? Or was it just the inclination to make everything mean something, to tie it all together?

There was always a moment in chemo, whether it was a physical or a psychological effect, when she felt clear and clean and above it all. That moment hit, and she felt sorry for Michael P, who wasn't doing well at all, and she felt sorry for the Bedazzler, who had to use tricks and games to get what she wanted. That kind of thing didn't make life better.

She looked around the room, at the auras resting around the patients in their chairs, their arms extended, hooked up and looking tolerant or resolved.

The room was vibrant with fear and determination, with people firmly believing there was more coming to them than the needles in their arms, the ice pops for sores, the ice caps for baldness, the pills for nausea, the fevers and fatigues, the lapping waves of death sneaking at their heels whenever they dropped their guard. It was a hateful place. If she could gather enough good memories, she could release them here. But it would only be a brief lull in their stay. A lull. An interruption. Would it be good enough? She began to experience that woozy feeling, the accumulation of the poisons in her blood. If only she could see Noah again, hear his voice, feel his hand on hers. Just a moment more of him. Two moments.

She missed Noah. She felt poor without more memories of Noah. They had never had enough time together.

And then something occurred to her. There was a way she could get more memories of Noah. She drew in her breath, surprised.

The color in the bottle was a butterscotch, a rich depth of color rather than the purity of, say, creamy yellow. Some colors Hildy could almost see through; some had denser aspects. The denser ones were a mix of feelings, she believed. She took a deep gulp.

"Mooshka, Mooshka, I'm hungry! I'd like an egg."

"Would you, my darling? Would you? A soft-boiled egg, maybe a slice of toast? And a strawberry, very nicely sliced?"

"Yes, yes, that sounds exactly right." It's a man's memory, and the man grabs Mooshka's arm and holds it close to him, looking up to her with a smile. "Dear Mooshka. Maybe two boiled eggs?" He watches his Mooshka, an attractive, stout woman with dark hair and a form-fitting dress, as she moves around the room, collecting eggs, bread, a pot, a toaster, a plate, a fork. She hums and stops to look at him a few times, just to smile at him. He is blessed. She is standing in sunlight.

Hildy can see by the cut of Mooshka's dress that it's the 1950s or early '60s. Her hair is teased and sprayed; the dress hugs her curves and spreads out in a swirl. The kitchen is avocado and pink. There are flowery curtains at the window.

Mooshka turns and swirls, and Hildy can hear the egg plop into the water, can hear the toaster knob being pushed down. There's a wonderful sense of peace and contentment, a lovely expectation of perfect eggs oozing on buttered toast. And Mooshka is a delight to watch; her movements are light and unhurried, as if when she touches anything, she is alive to its feel, its temperature and texture. Everything Mooshka does is replete with sensation. She folds and smoothes a napkin; she lifts the salt shaker and cups it in her hand to move it over in front of him; she pets the top of the butter dish. Mooshka's hair shines and her eyes crinkle, and she says, "It will just be a minute more, Mooshka," and Hildy realizes that they share a pet name, that the "sh" of Mooshka gives each of them pleasure. She gets the sense that they will someday wear clothes that look alike, shoes that bravely match. It's a beautiful thought, that these two people (and she is at least partially one of them, so she glows with the thought of it) will love each other so uncompromisingly that they will quite naturally become each other, that all the beauty and grace in she-Mooshka will be satisfied with whatever it is in he-Mooshka that she, too, finds relentlessly attractive.

Hildy tests it for a moment; what is attractive about he-Mooshka? He raises his hand to grasp the cup Mooshka hands to him; and his hand is lovely. Masculine, with little hairs on the fingers; the fingers are long, but they end in slightly spatulate fingertips. A little musical air is floating through his mind; he hums a stretch of it. He-Mooshka is a musician.

"That's lovely," his wife says.

"I'm writing it for you," he says agreeably. "A sonata for you. What can ever be as beautiful as you? Still, I'm going to do it. I look at you and always—always—there is music when I see you. The way you bend your arm, the way your hair moves, all of it, music."

"And here, sir—your egg!" she says in a throaty little whisper.

They laugh together, and Mooshka takes a fork to an egg and breaks the yolk.

It was a reverie, a daydream that made Hildy feel like she was floating, and it took a while before she drifted back to herself. She checked her notes on the bottle she'd just sampled and saw it belonged to an old man on a bench in the park. He was a dumpling of a man with fluffy white hair. Did he look like a lover, a composer? What a surprise it was to put this memory with him.

And then she realized that this particular memory was now no longer his; that she had stolen it and by doing so destroyed it, from his perspective.

But he must have more like this, she reasoned; he must have many mornings with Mooshka making him an egg; the memory was cozy and very familiar. It was a catchphrase of a memory. She made a note to herself: butterscotch; food prepared by beloved. She put a star next to it in her notes; find other butterscotch memories and see if she could reproduce the effect.

Cream, plum, lavender, sand, pewter, copper, wheat, lime, kelly green, aloe, teal, champagne, silver, tangerine, salmon, peach, fuchsia. She had to learn to break down the nuances of color in order to categorize them.

The thing about color was how often it got identified with food. Or things of nature. Of course, why wouldn't it? What should it be based on? Orange from oranges, lime from limes, lemon from lemons: how else would you identify these things? The color of sand, the color of wheat, the color of champagne; the color of flowers and fish and all the things of the earth and water. Aubergine. Tomato. Watermelon. How else would you name them?

What were the bad colors? She thought, at first, that the colors of fear, horror, regret, sorrow, anger, would all be the brash colors—red, acid green—but they weren't. Salmon, a lovely color, kept coming up sorrow. Spring green—the color of hope, she thought—was lethal anger. And when spring green shaded into the color of pine leaves, it wasn't a statement about the anger of spring green; it was a different kind of memory. Mostly to do with children or childhood. Spring green had a short range of paleness; and the darker end of it was no less violent than the lighter end.

She didn't know why the colors were that way. She was making progress in her inventory of shades, able to select good memories and bad, for the most part, but the colors themselves were so often broken into gradations (salmon had ten shades as far as she could determine) that she could make a mistake, on that gradation from salmon to harlequin rose. She kept trying to give each color a reasonable explanation, but why should there be a reasonable explanation? It just was.

It took dozens of tests before she began to see that the colors were linked; that each shade of salmon ran a thread throughout the aura, sometimes overlaid with yellow, sometimes with pink or red; sometimes the colors were layered one behind the other, so the resulting color to Hildy's eye was not the true color at all. It was a mix of two memories.

The salmon of sorrow tinged by the lavender of regret. One of her students (not Joey) was an older man who walked with a limp but who always smiled gently. She felt she could trust that smile not to get her into serious, troubling memories. She took some silver near his hip (which should have been his middle-age years), as she bent down to pick up a pencil she'd dropped. She hadn't sampled silver before; it was rare and usually just a sprinkle.

Silver was betrayal.

It was all about money. He was sitting at the table with his bank statements and a bunch of twenties, counting things up. As he counted, he recalled some of his victims (a memory within a memory!). An old couple he'd helped who trusted him to get him a new stove. A single mother who'd broken her hand and needed some repairs done on the car. Two friends from high school, who wanted to go in with him on starting a garage. His mother's savings account, which wouldn't matter to her because she was half-batty anyway. He left a few hundred dollars in the bank account, for some reason. Why? It was an odd thing to do; he had no conscience. Maybe it was a back door; if anything happened, if he got caught, he could always point to the bank accounts and maybe muddy things up.

If he had any doubts about his decision, it was all covered by the pleasure all the money gave him.

She thought about him as she went collecting time; how she would never have thought him a thief. He had been in love with money. Perhaps he still was. His love overrode everything and everyone. It was odd to see him in the classroom. He was learning about social media. What would he do with it? Should she try to sample his most recent time in order to see if he should be stopped, somehow, before repeating his behavior?

He made her uneasy; he made her feel uneasy about herself. Was what she had in mind a version of betrayal, a sneaky, greedy little binge? Was she a thief too?

The Bedazzler knocked on her door, entered, and walked straight over to the bottles of time. Of course they weren't *all* the bottles; Hildy had the good ones hidden all around the apartment, in cereal boxes, in boots, in the sleeves of jackets and coats. Anything on the table was problematic time; she'd sampled them and disliked what she'd found, so she put the "bad" jars and bottles out in the open.

"So you actually experience someone else's time?" the Bedazzler said, feigning ignorance. Her hand drifted over the tops of bottles, as if she were about to pick one.

"Yes. I'm sort of there with them, thinking. Seeing."

The Bedazzler picked one bottle up, looked at it, and put it back down. She turned to Hildy. "So you can remember their time? If you steal someone's time, even if they've forgotten it, you can remember it? Even afterwards?" She grinned.

"Yes," Hildy said. "As far as I know. Because I do write down notes, and I've noticed that I remember things, sometimes, and I can go back to check them and they're not my memories. I mean, not originally."

The Bedazzler got up abruptly, paced over to the window—the window where Hildy had so often seen Michael P standing under the lamplight. Was he there right now? She fought the urge to get up and check; that would give the Bedazzler some triumph over her, as if she had to see what the Bedazzler saw, as if she needed her.

The Bedazzler turned back, stopping at the table where Hildy's stolen bottles of time stood. The Bedazzler picked one up, tipping it back and forth. Hildy was sure she couldn't see any color in them, any depth, any texture. They appeared empty to people without the talent. The Bedazzler held it out. "How much time is in here?"

That question was always difficult for Hildy. "I don't know exactly. I think there may be differences in amounts of time; I don't know why. But the problem is that I always write down the time just before I open one, but I'm never able to write it down when I emerge. It's so hard to know when the bottled time stops. It gets looser and looser; it gets less and less, and I get more and more. But it's so gradual, and the transition is so interesting; I never manage to grab the idea of noting the time until much later. And you can think that when I *do* remember, maybe that's the real amount of time, but it varies by hours. I don't know. Anywhere from 30 minutes to two hours is my guess. Some hours are intense. Some hours are thinner. Does it represent how long those times felt to the person when they happened? Not all times seem the same."

It was so strange, how the two times overlapped and confused each other: the time that existed "really" for her, clouded by the time that existed from the bottle. If she said "an hour"—was that an hour of her existence; or was it an hour of memory time; and was the "real" time affected by the memory time? Why else would it prove impossible for her to record how long she actually experienced someone else's time?

The answer, of course, was to have someone else observe her; observe her time.

But how could someone else accurately observe her time? Because there was no objective way to say how much of her own time got used, since she believed she was mixed into the recalled time. Sure, an observer could note the time when she sniffed the bottle and the time when she said whatever word indicated she was back— but that would be the observer's time, wouldn't it? Hildy wouldn't be able to say how much of her own time had been used up; it was impossible to know that. Wasn't that why Michael P wanted the bottles? To add to his time?

"Tell me," the Bedazzler asked, turning back to her, "what are you doing with your bottles?"

"I'm trying to figure out what I'm seeing."

"That sounds like a very," she paused, "*clerical* job. I mean, you must be forced to use some kind of system to learn anything?"

"I'm making up the system as I go along."

"Not just names and dates? Or descriptions and dates?"

"Why are you asking? Is there something in particular you're looking for?"

The Bedazzler looked merry. "If I wanted to see what you had taken, say, from me—I wouldn't be able to find it out for myself?"

"Taken from you? No. I don't think you'd be able to figure it out. But, wait—do I have a bottle from you? Would you like to make a donation? Would you like to do it for the sake of science?" Hildy was acting. She *did* have one jar from the Bedazzler; but it was an early one, when her records weren't clear yet; she would love to take a bit more—a bit of that yellow over by her shoulder, indicating an event in the recent past that had a deep emotional tinge.

The Bedazzler stepped back and laughed. "Wouldn't you love that? Finding out what I intend to do—I always keep that to myself."

"No. Your past. Some spare remnant of time."

"None of my time is 'spare.'"

It was the middle of the night—gray time, if you were half-asleep or unable to stay asleep—and there must have been a noise, a sound, a vibration. Hildy was awake, the air almost checkered with night time, slightly buzzy with the dull thrum of electronics going about their business. She lay still, listening.

The window shade was down, but there were slits of light along the sides and at the bottom, and she could see, after a while, that the line of light on the right side was obscured slightly, and then went back to normal. It could be anything—a cloud, something passing in front of a window light or a street light—but Hildy began to picture the objects close to her. What could she lay her hands on, if it came to that?

The window was unlocked, and she'd never gotten around to getting gates installed. She was on the third floor; the ladder to the fire escape had been painted closed years ago; they all knew it. Someone would have to lower him- or herself down from another apartment window or from the roof. It was a quiet area, and no one was flashy-rich; robberies were rare; she had always felt safe.

Suddenly she didn't feel safe.

She was in the dark; the other person was in relative light; therefore blind when looking into Hildy's room. Hildy debated shouting—surely that would at least surprise the intruder? But did she want to warn him, give him a chance to consider his options? (Surely it was a "him"?) No; she'd rather keep the surprise going. She slowly inched her way out of bed and got to the far side, away from the window, close to her door.

She heard the window being slowly raised and saw an arm reach in, feel for a hold, then the other arm and a head followed.

Only one person. Slim, not too tall. Hildy's eyes had adjusted to the dark; the intruder would be blind. He was through the window.

She stood up, grabbed her lamp, and snarled, "I've got you, don't make a move!" She was surprised to hear herself: the ugly tones, the ridiculous statement. But it worked. The intruder froze for a split second, then pulled back, banging his head against the window. The head disappeared, then the arms.

Hildy rushed to the window, slamming it shut. Then she cursed herself and opened it to peer outside. She should know what the intruder looked like, shouldn't she? She should know if they ever met again. Her fear had dissipated, and she still had some adrenaline left because she felt strong and powerful. She was not a woman with cancer; she was a woman who had foiled a burglar, who had faced a new situation and overcome it. She was a superwoman.

She peered out and saw nothing, but heard footsteps running away. She looked left and right; nothing.

She turned on her lights and considered what to do. She would get gates as soon as possible. In the meantime, she jammed a broom diagonally across the window. Not a very good solution, but it would make a noise when it fell. She got kitchen chairs and upended them on the floor in front of the window; he wouldn't see them; he would get tangled. She was building a barricade, and it felt good.

She fell asleep after dawn, when there were noises on the street again—cars and people getting to work or walking their dogs or opening their doors and windows. It seemed unlikely that anyone would break in on her; she slept.

When she got up, she saw Michael P leaning against the building across the street, but his head was down and he wasn't staring at her window. Hildy grabbed her bag and ran down the stairs, her scarf flowing behind her.

She had just wrapped it on quickly, not tucking in edges. It felt like long hair; it felt good. It was also good to race down stairs; this was one of her healthy days.

It looked like Michael P had actually fallen asleep; he stood against the wall, his shoulders touching it. His head was bent down; his chin nestled on his neck; his eyes were closed. Hildy took out two small bottles and searched his aura; she wanted a color with a band inside it—but what color? Would it be a good or bad memory; something physical or mental or emotional? How long ago?

Anne had said there was a Michael there four years ago; the Bedazzler had said that Michael P had the book of meaning, whatever that was. He felt responsible for losing it—not physical time, then, emotional time. But there was the added complication of Molly, if there *was* a Molly. So something important, something to be guarded. She thought as fast as she could and settled on two spots, both of them what she judged to be lost memories. She took off the lid of one jar and dipped and lidded it, and put it away.

She had just taken off the lid of the second jar when he woke up suddenly, his eyes locking on her. He stiffened slightly, swallowed, then straightened up.

Hildy froze, then slowly put her hands down. "I was going to sample you," she said calmly.

His eyes slid down to the jar she held. He jerked away from her as if an electric shock had hit him. "Don't take my time," he hissed. "You can't take any of my time!"

"I didn't, I didn't," she said soothingly, ignoring her immediate feelings of guilt. She had to know; she had to find out.

His fingers gripping the wall, he began to inch away from her, then frowned and turned and slipped around the corner.

It had been necessary, hadn't it? How else would she find out what was going on?

She went back to her apartment, took the jar she'd filled up with Michael's time and set it on the windowsill. She sat next to it, opened his forgotten memory, and leaned back against her chair. The lighting was dim, so she turned on a lamp. There were little pools of brightness from the lampposts and from the streetlights as she walked down a street that was either cobbled or broken until she rounded the building and stopped briefly in front of an iron door.

"Molly?" she whispered, in Michael's voice. His hand reached up and opened the door.

Inside was a huge warehouse, with only a few pallets and a forklift at the far end. It was abandoned; there were rats scuttling—or something scuttling—away.

Hildy, remembering, sat in her chair, taken in by the memory, which had a sense of expectation in it, a sense of caution, a sense, way in the back of it, of desperation.

He moved across the cement floor toward a metal staircase going up to a second floor. Hildy heard the clang of his footsteps, felt the slight slipperiness of the stairs. This floor was lit by a small unshaded lamp, besides which was a table with a book on it.

"Molly? Where are you, Molly?"

He stood still and listened. A small creaking sound came from the right.

Hildy had a firm image of the building from Michael's jar of time—fairly firm. She could see the rows of windows, with their arched tops, the raised stones running down the corners of the building, the small setback from the street. A side driveway entered into an inner courtyard with loading docks. She couldn't see past it, though; she couldn't see other buildings or its location off an avenue, whether it was near the river or near a subway or park. She couldn't see the top of the building because it was dark; so she couldn't see what buildings stood behind it and thereby figure out downtown or uptown, east side or west side. It could even be Brooklyn or Queens, she reasoned. There were no clues.

But behind one of the darkened windows, a faint light had bloomed and shifted as he looked up, and she wanted to find it and see what it hid. Michael's heart had been racing lightly, with anticipation, not fear; whatever was in there was what Michael was searching for.

She should have taken more time from him; she was thinking about that when she realized she was out of his time. She didn't want to forget what she had seen: she searched through her apartment till she found paper, then she sat down and drew it in as best she could.

Brick warehouse; partial wording on the lintel with the name of the company—all she had seen was "ck Company." Googling that gave her thousands of answers, but nothing helpful.

She looked out her window and saw a lonely corner; Michael P wasn't there. She should show the drawing to him; maybe he would remember.

But if she'd taken that bit of memory, what would he be capable of remembering?

Behind it all, of course, she had cancer. The chemo came and took her over and then released her, and with any luck at all, the chemo would kill the cancer. Her numbers were good: every time she came in for an infusion they did a check of the antibodies that indicated whether cancer was in her system. She was bald and without eyebrows, and her numbers were good. Ahead of her lay a time when the chemo would stop. Would she be able to see the auras then?

Even if she couldn't, she would know they were there, of course. It struck her as strange that Michael P had seen the auras but hadn't blindly scooped out time around people. She would if she needed to.

She wondered if she would forget that she could do it: wasn't Michael P's problem that he forgot? Maybe he hesitated because he thought there was something else involved.

So it might change for her as it had changed for him. She hated the idea of that.

It was raining that day, but the next day was cloudy — a good day to rent a bicycle and start going up and down the streets in Manhattan, looking for the right warehouse. Of course, it might be Brooklyn, or Queens, or even New Jersey — she hadn't seen any landscape to identify it. She would start with Manhattan.

She packed water and rubbed on sunscreen, and took a sweater and some chocolate bars and rode out to West Street, deciding to go up to midtown first, then double-back and go down, around the Battery and up the East Side. She bought a pair of binoculars.

She stopped off in the West Village, in Chelsea, got as far as 42nd Street and decided there was nothing up there, and turned around. A lot of the industrial buildings had been converted into residential; nothing looked right as she crept in and out of the two streets nearest the river. She stopped once for a break and took her binoculars and peered across the river—but there was nothing that caught her interest in Hoboken.

She turned around and went slowly below Houston Street, past some huge facilities and areas that just seemed too visible. She saw nothing until she came up the curve around the island and neared South Street. Seaport. Here there were warehouses—old, dirty, decrepit. Her heart rose. She got off the bike when the streets were cobblestoned; it was better to look slowly, anyway, because there were a few buildings behind buildings. But then she remembered the large driveway and the inner open courtyard and realized a quick glance would tell her all she needed to know.

She was so sure she'd find the right place, but there was nothing she could make fit with her memory—his memory. She walked over to a pier above the Seaport, sitting down and thinking. She took her binoculars out and studied the shoreline of Brooklyn, snaking her eyes along. Yes, there were plenty of warehouses. She remembered passing Industry City once, on her way to somewhere else on the Gowanus Expressway. That had a promising ring.

By late afternoon she was panting; she took a taxi home, jamming the bike into the rear seats and sitting in the front.

She tipped a lot, yanked the bike out, went upstairs to her apartment, and collapsed. The name "Industry City" kept squiggling in her mind. Filled with warehouses, many of them abandoned, she believed.

She woke up near midnight, hungry. She smelled spaghetti sauce cooking; she heard someone in the kitchen. Her heart pounded at first, but then she began to be angry. Who said she couldn't have some privacy? Why did they decide that locks meant nothing when it came to Hildy? How dare they?

She rose, hungry and righteous, and found the Bedazzler in the kitchen. She had already put the spaghetti into the boiling water, and the tomato sauce bubbled merrily. The table was set. There were olives and grated cheese and a loaf of Italian bread. And a green salad.

Hildy scowled and sat down. "I'll kill you later," she said gruffly. "After dinner."

The Bedazzler drained the pasta, put a little olive oil on it, and brought it to the table, then poured the sauce into a bowl, brought that as well, and sat down.

"You must be exhausted," she said. "How many miles do you think you biked today?"

Hildy ladled sauce over the pile of spaghetti she'd moved onto her plate. She took tablespoons of grated cheese. "I don't understand all the connections," she said, after chewing her first forkful. "Were you married to Michael P? Why are you following him? And what do you want—that's the big one. I don't know what anyone wants."

The Bedazzler sighed. "You keep looking for a mystery," she said, serving herself. "I wonder if you've noticed that? But here are a few obvious things: you can see time, you can steal time. You're learning to recognize the colors of time. You might lose the ability if you continue treatment or if you stop treatment—it's unpredictable. If you do, then it's just over. And you wonder why people want something from you." She lifted her hand up and pointed to her own chin, obviously mimicking a foolish Hildy. "Oh, I can steal time? But what do you *want* from me?"

Hildy's chewing slowed down; the weakness she'd felt when she woke up had gone away. She ate some of her salad and buttered some bread. "All right," she said after a minute. "I have a talent. But both you and Michael P are interested in this ability not just to get more time, but as a tool to get something else." She took a sip of water. "Molly." She took another sip. "The Book of Meaning." She put her glass down. "And I don't know if Molly is real."

"Molly is real."

"Or if the book is real."

The Bedazzler shrugged. "He says it's real. Why wouldn't it be?"

And Hildy grinned now, a mean grin. "Stolen memories," she said. "If anyone else has ever done any mixing and matching, then who can say where the true memories belong? You might have lost your own or you might have sniffed part of someone else's memory."

There was a long pause then. The Bedazzler studied the wall behind Hildy, then nodded. "Michael P is dying," she said. She clasped her fingers together, placing her hands on the table. "You can help him by giving him time—the right kind of time, of course. No more tricks with gray time. Give him clean time, pure time. You can help people like the Baldies, who are running out of time. Is that worthwhile? Do you have anything better to do with your life?" Her elbows twitched a little into her sides, just briefly, and then relaxed.

Hildy could feel a blush rising on her neck, but why was she blushing? All she knew was that everyone she'd met lately wanted something from her. And they all knew something she didn't—maybe just little pieces of something, but what they told her and what they withheld from her were both for their benefit, not hers. "Half of what you say is a lie. I just don't know which half. What should I believe?"

She pulled her lips back; she wanted to show her teeth. Maybe it was some primitive action; she didn't care. She felt like an animal being tracked, leaving scents and broken twigs for all to find, ignorant herself of scents and broken twigs.

The Bedazzler stared at her thoughtfully. She released her hands and put them flat on the table. "You have an illness," she began. "Michael P had the same illness. And yes, we were married, for a while. The thing about your illness is that it has odd twists to it; it's so rare that it's hard to know which twists belong to it and which belong to the individual. I learned certain things when my husband was ill, but how would I know if they're true for everyone? I learned that he could look at people and see their memories, their lost memories; that he could see the time they had behind them. He said he could see the time they had ahead of them as well. And then it turned out that Michael was dying, and he needed the time. He tried to be responsible; he tried. And then suddenly he could see the time but he couldn't take it and what was the point of that? It moved away from him, he said; he was never quick enough to grab it. Eventually he couldn't even see it. I have a theory," she said, standing up and walking to a window, where she pulled back the curtain and stared out. Was she expecting to see Michael P?

"Here's the thing. Michael is running out of time. And he doesn't remember the things he did when he could see time. He knows something's wrong; he's not sure what it is. I don't want him to suffer." Her voice should have cracked on that last line, Hildy thought.

The Bedazzler leaned towards Hildy. Her eyes were sharp and her voice was firm. "I need you to help me with this. You need to get him some time. And you need to find out what he's forgotten."

Hildy answered slowly. "He's got lots of forgotten memories. We all do. Most of our time is forgotten, when you think about it. It would be hard to find exactly the right memory."

"I know you can see it," the Bedazzler hissed. "I know you can do it. I don't want to hear excuses. You have a talent for seeing time; I have a talent for coming and going like a shadow. So just know that I can come in while you're asleep and cut your throat." She caught Hildy's twitch of surprise. "I'd hate to do it, but you know how emotional women can be." She smiled grimly.

"Of course," Hildy said, trying to make her heart go back to normal. The Bedazzler had just changed from being annoying to being dangerous. "I see. Well, that's an incentive. It surely is. I'll have to find what I can from his aura. Are you sure there isn't something you've forgotten that would be helpful?" She turned shakily—how she wanted to appear unmoved, and how difficult that was—and picked up a few more jars. "Maybe Michael P actually told you something and you've forgotten it? Some piece of information you thought was unimportant? It could happen, of course, something slipped out while something more important occupied your mind."

"I'm sure I would remember."

"Tell me the last time you saw Molly."

Hildy circled her very slowly, observing all the colors, all the gradations. The Bedazzler's face had changed and was now frozen into longing. Her body stiffened and leaned slightly forward.

"I was walking down the hallway," the Bedazzler said. Her eyes looked off to the distance. "I can't place the hallway. Where were we living then? Or was I visiting someone? That's the last memory I have of her. She had a wonderful smile, a smile that could change the world." Her head sunk down briefly, then she lifted it up and glared at Hildy. "You have to find her."

"Are you sure there's a child? You hesitated; you couldn't remember where you were. Are you sure it's not just someone else's memory? I could try to find out." She held out a jar.

The Bedazzler slapped her, hard. Hildy was knocked off balance. "I remember her!" the Bedazzler spat out in a croak. "I remember her! She's real! She's mine!" She stood still for a moment, glaring and catching her breath. She looked into Hildy's eyes, furious, and then her own eyes backed away. She shivered, took up her bag, and walked out the door.

Hildy watched her from the window, rubbing her stinging face. She could see the Bedazzler's shoulders, held tight; her head forced upwards. Her body language had changed. Hildy was sure the Bedazzler was worried about whether Molly truly existed. So much of her thoughts were spent on ruses and manipulations, all to get Molly back—it would of course be unbearable if she, in turn, were manipulated into believing something that wasn't true, something that mattered to her enormously, and yet wasn't true.

The problem was, if the liars didn't even know they were lying, if the memories she could manage to sample weren't originally *their* memories—how was she to proceed?

Hildy walked over to study her vials and jars and her embroidered man—that skeleton with the colored pieces of paper floating around him. Was there a special color for a memory that had been introduced into someone else—a false memory? She thought about it. Was it a false memory, once it was part of your memories? Why would it look different? In the same way that food became part of your body, air became part of your body, wouldn't a memory, once settled in, become as much of your time as anything else? In a sense, weren't all memories outside the realms of true and false? If anyone could recall something, no matter how delusional, did it matter to that person whether it was false? It would take the same emotional toll either way, and wasn't that all that really remained—the emotions?

And why did the truth suddenly matter so much? Her affair with Noah had depended on a lie (implicitly, to his wife, but also implicitly to herself). She had valued Noah above the truth. She shook her head wearily. She had taken what she could and faced the consequences. And that meant that there was no one beside her when she faced her diagnosis. Her world had ended up empty. She had been too selfish. But now there was this new world, filled with things she didn't know and had trouble figuring out. How was she to navigate it? What use would she make of it?

She knew that she desperately wanted to understand it all—Molly, the Book, what she should do with time. But if the Bedazzler believed something, and didn't know how she came to believe something, then what would protect Hildy against the very same thing? She was subject to memories as well. What memory could sabotage her? She looked in the mirror, studying herself. She had no hair or eyebrows; therefore the cancer was real. And she looked middle-aged, so she was probably as old as she thought. She lifted her head to look around her apartment.

Jars, the embroidered man; it all looked real. She knew, for instance, that her memory of the warehouse was not an original memory, though she had to keep that hanging in the front of her mind, since it was part of her memory now. That was a hard thing to do, but she still could do it. So she had taken time from Michael, and there was something in a warehouse, probably not anything to do with Molly, but something that would make sense of the Bedazzler and Michael P both, since both of them were urging her on, in their own ways.

All of it was weird and special; all of it centered around her; they all believed she was capable of doing this thing, this strange impossible thing. She just didn't know it herself.

⚬

She still continued to collect time, slowly and carefully, and only from those she thought were healthy. And she collected memories, too, a few happy memories, because she wanted some relief from feeling pressured and alone. She was a block from home when she saw a man approaching her from the opposite direction. He shambled closer, and she saw that his clothes were torn and hanging on him, and that the left half of his face was one open sore.

She moved out of his way.

He continued to move past her, slowly, his awful face looking forward.

Her first reaction had been to cross the street. She was going through chemo; her immune system was shot. But she felt a sudden dreadful sympathy for him. There was something wrong with him, and here she was, a person with her own awful disease, refusing to help. How could she refuse to help? Was that a cancer on his face? Was it like the cancer in her head, the cancers eating the Baldies—the cancers that were her community, in fact?

What could she do to help, really? She had her bag of time, that was all she had.

She looked back at him. His walk was slow and automatic. Joyless, mindless, crushed.

She put her bag down, looked through it, and took out the two jars she was saving for herself, the good memories. She could at least give him that, some false but lovely moments. Would he sniff them? She took out some singles and rolled them into two sticks. She lifted the snap lids the smallest amount she could and stuck the money in. He would open them to get the money. Of course he would.

She went back toward him, and followed him for a moment, and then called out softly, and handed him the jars. He stopped, held his hand out, looked at the jars, and then moved on, still carrying them.

She moved off as well. She was ashamed of herself. She had tried to ignore him because of the great wound on his face, the shredded clothing. Would she have dealt with that kind of pain the way he seemed to—blindly, silently, robotically? She couldn't dismiss him as some kind of crazy homeless man because she too felt isolated by her illness.

What were her options? Should she give time to people who were running out? That homeless man? She was right to give him a couple of good jars, though she had no idea how much it would ultimately matter to him. Maybe he had shut out the world and that would include those times she gave him. Wasted? Maybe.

Was she the kind of person who could decide who deserved what?

She had to turn away from this for a while. She was not a hero. She had been headed for an ordinary life.

⟐

She went to the park around noon a day later, looking for the Baldies. They were huddled around cardboard cups of coffee and a box of donuts, under the trees above Sheep's Meadow.

"Did you find anything out about Michael P and the Bedazzler?" Hildy asked.

"Don't you want a donut first?" Grace asked. "Don't you want to ask how we are?" She looked haggard and angry.

Hildy nodded. "I was rude. How are you?"

"We lost Rob." The group drew a little closer. "It was a surprise. We all thought he had more time."

They were alike in the look they gave her, an unforgiving one.

"I forgot to come back until now," Hildy said. "I'm so sorry."

"You forgot?" Grace asked bitterly. "You forgot?" Her mouth was thin and hard.

Hildy knew there was no good argument. She waited, hanging her head for a minute, then said, "I don't understand what's going on, so it's hard for me to know what to do. Or why to do it."

"Save us," Grace said. "That's simple, isn't it? Start from there." A few of the others nodded, but most of them now began to look away. They'd judged her.

"I can't get you enough time, you know. I can't possibly get all of you all of the time you need."

This was greeted with silence. It was a brutal thing to say, certainly; but, really, how was she supposed to save everyone?

She felt a little irritated at that thought— "saving." She was not a missionary! She sighed. "I have to figure out what to do. Should I steal people's time? Isn't that basically killing them earlier? Or does it have nothing to do with that—how does it work? I can't just go around grabbing, now can I?"

"You've been collecting time all along, haven't you?" Grace asked. "How do you justify that?"

"That's the point," she said, exasperated. "I've been working in the dark. I didn't know. But now I know that I'm affecting them. How can I keep doing it? The ones who want me to go on are the ones who want something from me—time, or information." She threw her hands up. "This is incredible, how no one has any doubts about what I should do! They tell me what they want, and I can't get any information out of anyone."

"I found something out," Grace said finally. She eyed Hildy carefully. "I know where Michael P goes, most of the time. It's an area near the old shipyards."

"In Brooklyn?" Hildy asked, suddenly charged. She should have gone to Brooklyn! She had thought it was Manhattan because she thought Michael P was in Manhattan. A fly buzzed by her ear and she raised a hand to swat it away.

"Carl followed him there. I did too." Grace watched Hildy. "I didn't know how to reach you. So I waited. You wanted us to get you some information, and we got it. He just wanders around along Second Avenue by the old trolley tracks. He never seems to find what he wants."

The fly landed on Grace's shoulder. Hildy looked at it; the fly had an aura, a small, visible aura. It horrified her. She felt, all at once, an unbearable sadness for all of life.

"I'm sorry," Hildy said. "I really am. I should have come sooner. I know it. It's been very confusing." She stopped herself. Excuses wouldn't help. "I'll do what I can," she said finally, and left. She had no idea what that meant, "I'll do what I can." Everyone wanted her to get time for *them;* they wanted her to get information for *them*. She couldn't refuse because they were dying—she couldn't refuse, could she? But what was the cost of all this? What would it take from her?

Hildy rented a car and drove to Brooklyn—it was late afternoon, but it didn't matter what time it was on the Gowanus; it was always crowded and slow. She got off the exit before Industry City, past the newly greened Brooklyn Bridge Park. It spread out next to the water; she went inland an avenue or so.

There were old warehouses and decrepit buildings here. She drove up and down, always looking at the view down the streets to the bay. Was it a bay? She should have gotten a better map. She took it out and marked the streets as she drove them, stopping at corners, considering angles and views. If she came from a different direction, how different would the view be? She backtracked and compared a few streets as she came from the opposite direction. No; it wasn't all that different; she would know it when she saw it.

Industry City took longer; there were so many possibilities. But the neighborhood was right: lost, abandoned, or not abandoned but ignored. No one had gentrified it; the trash and the hulking parked vehicles sat largely indifferent to atmosphere, unless the atmosphere was decrepit and desolate, which it did well enough.

And then there it was.

There was the arch above the doorway, a sign completing the letters she'd seen: National Clock Company. There was an abandoned trolley line nearby, huge warehouses, cobblestone streets. All of it struck her as exactly right, even if she hadn't noticed the trolley line or the cobblestones in her memory. They had been in the back of her mind. *His* mind.

It was sliding close to evening, shadows snaking across the street, and the warehouse stood stolidly close up to the gutter, with barely a sidewalk. There were truck bays and large doors and small ones, and she could see a light on the second floor. A brief shadow showed at a grimy window and went away. Another light went on.

Who was waiting inside? Was it dangerous? She wasn't helpless, but chemo had taken its toll, physically and mentally. And what would she say when she met whoever was inside? "Do you know why I'm here?" was the only reasonable question—she certainly didn't know why she was there; and if she didn't know, why should anyone else? And yet it seemed part of some plan. A good plan, a bad plan?

She knocked on the nearest door, then tried the handle. Locked. She tried the loading platform, which had a short flight of steps and a door next to it. Locked. She tried all the doors facing the street, then walked around the building to the back. There was an alley here, with garbage and, she assumed, rats, but there was also a wooden door with two glass panes, and a dim light shining through them. This door was open.

Inside was another door leading to the warehouse floor—locked—and a wooden stairway, which she went up slowly, listening to the stairs squeak. Was it good that they squeaked? She didn't want to surprise anyone, certainly; but maybe it was better not to advertise her entrance? It didn't matter, really. She was surprising herself more than anyone else.

No door at the top, just a doorway. The room she entered was very large, with wooden plank flooring. There was one bulb hanging from the ceiling, about ten feet high. Weak sunlight made her eyes unable to adjust easily to the lighting, so she squinted as she moved cautiously toward the weak bulb in the center of the room. Beneath it sat a woman with a crocheted hat of many colors. She sat in a clear area about 100 feet square; all around that were boxes stacked high—no, not boxes. They were plastic crates with one side missing; they were stacked so the open side faced the center of the room.

The woman got up without a word and walked toward Hildy, who stiffened and stepped aside.

"The lights," the woman said, amused. She reached out to a switch on the wall, and dozens of fluorescent overhead lights flickered on.

Hildy looked around. All the boxes were filled with water bottles.

"Time," the woman said, following Hildy's eyes. "Those are all filled with good, solid time. High quality, no gray time. No bad memories."

"Then it must have been somebody's future," Hildy murmured. "Many people's future?"

"Just a little bit here and there. Nothing to get all moral about. I can show you how to be even more selective about time: how to take a little here and there, adding it up, so maybe someone loses a few hours, but no one gets cheated out of a lifetime. How to avoid the pearly time that sticks it all together. Did you figure it out? The pearly time is the unused time."

"Their future?" Yes, she had wondered about that. She had tried to stick to the colored time, interested in what it held. She was glad she had been careful about the future.

"Yes. Though, you know, not everyone gets to use it all up." The woman had a calm, authoritative voice.

Hildy stared at the bottles; she couldn't calculate how many bottles were there, or how much time was there—but it was a lot. Thousands of bottles, maybe tens of thousands.

"Would you like some?"

Hildy looked at the woman closely. She was old—her skin was dry and had deep creases—but she was straight-backed and commanding. She wore a gray tunic over loose three-quarters pants—some kind of yoga clothing? She had a half-length magenta sweater over her tunic and a thick necklace of varicolored ceramic beads. She looked like some throwback to the '60s, actually; her hair was long and parted in the middle and had thin ornamental braids framing her face.

"Who are you?" Hildy asked. She tried to keep an eye on the woman as she looked around. There was another door at the far end and more light showing around its frame. A few of the large windows had been cleaned, the ones looking out on the water. The chair the woman had been sitting in was actually comfortable-looking. It seemed ergonomic. And she had a table next to it, with a large book and a cup of coffee. Hildy could smell the coffee.

"I'm Molly. You've been looking for me." The woman laughed at that.

Hildy turned away, looking again at the bottles of time. The Baldies would of course be grateful for them. Michael P needed them desperately. If this was all clean time, it would be a miraculous thing for all of them. But Molly…this was more confusing than not. The Bedazzler searching for her child—it could hardly be this woman. She could be the Bedazzler's mother or grandmother—it was hard to judge her age, exactly. Her body was so much more supple than her face.

"I can choose time very accurately," Molly said. "I can show you how to do that, how to pinpoint the memories and categorize them as to emotion and time and even place. Would you like that?" She peered at Hildy. "You've gotten very far on your own, if you've made it here. But there's so much more I can show you." She bowed quickly. "I can be your guide."

"Why?" Hildy asked. "What would you show me?" She stopped there; she had too many questions. And she needed to find a way of asking them coherently.

"You've noticed you can read auras—I mean, not just the colors and the variants, but sometimes you can see how thin they are? How they seem to be fading?"

Hildy's heart suddenly thudded; it seemed irregular and stumbling; it was a terrible, disquieting feeling. Her eyes went distant; she felt herself curl up inside like an armadillo. She knew what was coming.

"Your aura is getting thin. That happens when the future, the pearly vein of future time, starts mixing in. Leaking. Of course it's hard to see in yourself; but it's not impossible. I think you've noticed, haven't you? Or suspected?"

Hildy pulled her eyes over to the woman. "You don't know that for sure," she said. She hoped she'd said it coldly; she wanted to be cold, indifferent. Unpersuaded.

"If you don't believe it about yourself, then there are all those people you know who need more time," Molly continued. "Especially Michael P. I'm afraid Michael P is—" She let a sweeping gesture end her sentence.

"Who are you?" Hildy asked, her voice too loud. "What is this? What do you want?"

"Well, to be exact, I want *you*. You should have figured that much out. But what do you think this is?" she asked, sweeping her hand around the room, indicating all the rows of bottles.

"I don't know."

Molly sighed. "I guard the time. I give it, and I take it—oh, I'm not God, not at all, I'm just someone in a line of guardians. Time gets given and taken so haphazardly. We try to rectify that; we try to take from the ones who are given too much and hand it to the ones who need it most. There are a handful of us, spread far apart, and it's an impossible job. We can't make everything fair. But without us, there's no spot on earth where anyone tries to even it out. It's a bit of holiness, this business of giving time out to the ones who deserve it. And I can't leave here, of course."

"Why not?"

"I ran out of my own time years ago. But one of the privileges of my position is that I can loosen up time in here, just open up jars as I need them. Loose time. I can live as long as I stay here and breathe it. That's why I need someone else, you see: someone to take time and give time, outside, out there." She walked to one of the clean windows and gazed outside. "Come look at my world."

Hildy came next to her cautiously; she wasn't sure what this woman planned on doing, or what was involved. But she stood there comfortably, her hands crossed on her stomach, and Hildy looked out the window too.

The window showed the harbor. Below them was the end of a street, which just petered out to a tiny parking area, a railing, a path half-dirt and half-concrete leading away to a long pier where one man was fishing. Closer, below them, and across the wide alley, was another warehouse, smaller and more compact. In front of it were two cats, very fat and very comfortable. There were bowls of water and opened cans of cat food arranged around them.

"Felix and Fineboy," Molly said. "They've gotten too fat. They used to stalk things—mice, rats, pigeons—but now they just wait patiently. Sometimes they go for a walk, but their bellies swing, and that must be annoying. Fineboy has to step around his belly, it hangs down so much. There are actually two women who come and feed them; they take turns; they cover for each other. When it flooded here, I opened one of the doors, and they climbed on some pallets."

Her attention switched to an old man sitting at a table near the railing. "He reads palms. Not very good, I don't think, or at least that's what I've been told. But occasionally he hits his mark."

"There don't seem to be very many people here."

"He told me once he only requires a palm a week."

"Requires?"

"For his profession, for his identity. We all have an identity, no?" She looked closely at Hildy, her eyes expecting some recognition of the wisdom of that statement.

"And your identity is that you're a guardian of time," Hildy said flatly.

Molly nodded. "Michael P helped me for a while, but he was affected by his disease, or even his treatment; he began to fail. Before he got too far, I had him give the Bedazzler some memories; and I helped him find you. I dropped bread crumbs for you, you see, by mixing some memories together for her and for him. Or memories of breadcrumbs!" Like an actress, she clapped her hands together and lifted her chin and gave a dramatic laugh.

Hildy's eyes strayed to the large book on Molly's table. "Michael P mentioned a book. The meaning of life, he said. Is that it?"

Molly grinned. "Not exactly. Not really. The map of time, perhaps?"

Hildy was startled.

"It's my own research on what the colors mean. And of course it's the catalog of the bottles themselves, based on the colors. Plus my system for knowing where I've stored the different kinds of time." She waved her hand at the aisles of bottles. "I'm proud of how organized it all is. It's useful, of course. I can find whatever I need quite easily."

"Yes," Hildy said. "Of course. I have a system too." She thought of her cards, her codes, the skeleton with all the numbers on it. She could see how it was all fitting in, or most of it. Not all of it.

"You made the Bedazzler believe Michael P had lost her child?" It sounded preposterous to Hildy; and a little roundabout. Why not give her a memory that explained it all instead?

"It was insurance. I found a memory that I thought would come in useful, back when I was sampling—I imagine you're still sampling, yes? I thought so. I came across a memory of a stolen child, and I mixed it with one of Michael P's memories of coming here to see me. Have you tried mixing yet? It takes some practice. You can falsify a memory, and you can find that false memory. It will have the color of a lost memory but a little rosier. It will catch the eye, that little extra touch of rose."

"Yes," Hildy said, thinking back. "I've seen that. But why did you do it?"

"Michael was losing his abilities. I needed someone to find me—I needed the next person to find me." She squinted at Hildy. "That's you. I need someone to replace Michael P.

"You're very special. You have a gift, a rare one. You can take time, and you can give time. You're valuable. I can use your services. And in return, I can teach you a bit more than you know right now. You're making guesses about this color and that, this pattern and that. It can take you years to get it straight—if you have years." She paused, and her lips gave just a hint of a smile. "You do have time left, but not as much as you want. More than Michael has, probably. He was in terrible shape the last time I saw him. Forgetting things. Getting lost."

"You can help him," Hildy pointed out. "Give him some of this time." She gestured down the rows.

"Oh, I can't *give* it to him." Molly laughed and gestured towards the crates of bottles. "I can't leave. I told you, I live on loose time now. I ran out of my own many years ago. I've been opening time as I need it, and I can't take the chance of being away from my resources."

Hildy stared at all the boxes, all the bottles. "I can't imagine how many people this represents. You took all this time from someone else?"

"Well, not the same person, obviously. A little here, a little there. Time lost on lines, time waiting for appointments, time spent in traffic—why, people lose time without counting it up or noting how much is subtracted. I do the same thing—or did the same thing. Fifteen minutes, an hour: do you think that would matter in your life? That's what I do. I accumulate. I can even spare a little now, if you join me. Those Baldies, for instance, or Michael P— there are people you can share with. Think of yourself as a kind of Robin Hood. Take it away from those who have too much; give it to those who have too little."

A bit grandiose, Hildy thought. Maybe more than a bit.

But she looked at all the crates, at all the bottles within the crates. "Who brings them to you if you can't go out?" she asked.

"Ah," Molly said. "The fly in the ointment. It used to be Michael P. I saw him beginning to get confused, so I made a special mixed memory and told him to give it to the Bedazzler. The memory of a child being stolen right out front. Did you find it? No? Well, it was powerful stuff," she said. "I did it in case Michael P failed to remember where I was and who I was. The Bedazzler held my backup clue. Remember, if I die, it all dies. Look at all those bottles, all this reservoir." She nodded at her stacks of time. "Think of what can be done with it."

She thinks she's a god, Hildy told herself. Her ears were open and her eyes were open and she was thinking rapidly. It would be good to be generous; it would be good to be able to choose time more exactly. Thoughts flew through her head: saving Michael P, saving the Baldies. Saving herself.

Someone was banging on the door downstairs. Molly's eyes widened and then narrowed. She moved quickly to another window and peered down. "You've been followed," she said. "You weren't very clever, after all."

"Followed? Who would follow me? And what difference would it make?"

Molly turned angrily away. "I don't suppose you have a gun?" she asked, her eyes sweeping around the room. "No, never mind; a gun would be too messy."

Hildy heard steps tapping their way furiously up the stairs. Molly looked irritated rather than frightened, so she didn't really think there was any danger. There was nothing to do but peer expectantly.

Three people came in, their eyes automatically taking in the whole room.

"What are you doing here?" Hildy asked, surprised.

Anne, the chemo nurse, smiled at her sweetly. "I've always wanted to come here someday. Who needs a middleman, after all? It's so much simpler to set it up directly."

The acupuncturist agreed easily. "Michael P liked to make his appointments a little stagey."

"Would he show or wouldn't he?" the swami agreed. "As businesses go, not the best way to build a loyal clientele."

"I'm lost," Hildy confessed.

Molly stood stiffly by the window, her eyes flicking from face to face. "Buying and selling time is a very lucrative business," she said coldly. "Michael P was very good at finding contacts, at delivering time, good time, to his customers. And I imagine the three of you made a fair amount off what he gave you?" Molly spat out her words.

"It's a service," Anne said, shrugging. Her voice, Hildy noted, still sounded soothing and gentle.

"I'm sure you wouldn't want to keep it all for yourself," the swami said. "Terribly unenlightened."

"So this is all illegal?" Hildy asked. The sudden interruption, the surprise revelations—all of this had an element of noir to it: a fractured, off-kilter noir.

Molly rolled her eyes and hooked her arms across her chest. She stuck a foot out and shifted her weight. "I don't imagine there are any laws about it. There's a limited number of people who are even capable of believing—"

"Mostly the ones who need to believe," Anne said. "I can tell who they are. They get told that their tumors are still growing, despite the chemo, and they ask me if I've heard of anything else. They're the ones who want to find something, who are willing to take a chance—of course, why wouldn't they? Their life is a risk. And let me just say, too, that I'm glad I can help them."

"As am I," the swami said. "My own personal faith involves being both realistic and charitable—to take your share and share what's left. If I have enough time for myself and the ability to get more time for those who need it, why then, it would be wrong to withhold what I can get."

"We're all very practical," the acupuncturist agreed. "Balance; balance. It's necessary for the individual and also for the universe. I am dedicated to restoring what has become injured or neglected. It was a great discovery, this ability to mete out time. You can't just start it and then stop; there are people who depend on it. Of course it's a business; there is no harm in a business if its goal is to help people, as we do; the harm is in withdrawing the help, in making it disappear." He leaned toward Molly. "We need a steady supply of time. You've stopped getting it to us. That's unpleasant for our business connections."

"She can't leave here," Hildy said. "And Michael P lost track of everything. You can't blame her for that."

"No?" Anne murmured. She stepped up to Molly. "Is there something wrong? Some reason why you can't leave?"

"I'm guarding all of this. You say you want this as a product; well, it's valuable. Someone has to watch it."

Anne walked over to the nearest crate. "I don't understand," she said. "How are you protecting it? If I wanted to take, say, a dozen bottles of time…. You don't mind if I use that bag there, do you? Just to make it easier to carry." She took the bag, filled it with bottles, shook them into place and turned back to Molly. "Well, guardian, aren't you going to do something?"

"Put that down," Molly said sternly.

The swami laughed. "This is one of those philosophical problems, isn't it? If a guardian has no power, what can she really guard?"

The acupuncturist nodded and began to move down a row of crates. "She's really just an advisor, I think. Advising us of what she guards. Semantics."

"Semiotics, I think," Hildy said. She was still trying to figure out the big picture. If Molly guarded the bottles (and yes, could it be called guarding?), and Michael P brought her bottles of time (why?), and the others bought the time and distributed it—well, there was nothing wrong here, was there? She had done the same thing on a smaller scale. It was all goods and services, wasn't it?

"Back here," the acupuncturist called from down the row. "These are all empty."

Immediately, Anne and the swami became alert and went down other rows. "These are good!" the swami shouted, and he was answered by Anne's cry, "All empty! All of them!"

They scurried back and forth along the rows, calling out their findings. Clearly, half the warehouse was empty—maybe more.

Molly stood stiffly alone, her eyes on Hildy. Hildy was aware of it, but her mind was working hard. Of course there would be empty bottles; Michael P had been the supplier, and he had stopped bringing time. Molly had opened up the bottles because she needed time, and they hadn't been refilled.

The obvious conclusion was that she, Hildy, was the pivotal person in the room. The only one who could see time, and the only one who could fill those empty bottles.

Molly's sharp eyes watched her, and Hildy rearranged her face, trying to seem ignorant or not directly involved. But it was an inevitable conclusion; they would all reach it, and indeed Anne was already approaching her thoughtfully.

"Hildy," Anne called out gently. "Hildy, can I talk to you?"

The acupuncturist came running down an aisle, stopping only when he reached Molly. "You'll pay for this!" he shouted. "You're using them up, aren't you? Michael P told me that. I can turn a blind eye when there's more and more of it, but I have orders to fill, orders that have been paid for and waiting for months now, months!" His voice cracked a little on the last words, and his mouth twisted. Molly said nothing, and this made him angrier. "You'll pay for this! You'll pay or else—" He couldn't think of a threat immediately. Instead, he reached down to a piece of metal on the floor (an old window crank, Hildy thought) and he raised it up and threw it.

It smashed the window. Molly gasped; she pulled the half-sweater close around herself and moved back into the room, away from the air that came through the window.

Loose time was contained in the warehouse; the broken window would make it escape, Hildy realized. Wasted time.

The acupuncturist broke another window. "Stop, Lew," Anne said sharply. "That won't help. It won't help anyone."

"They'll be after me," Lew answered, panting. "You don't know; I've gotten into them for too much now. I'm ruined."

"Stop it!" Anne cried.

While they began to argue with each other, Molly turned and strode down the rows, tumbling crate after crate of time, stamping on them. She wasn't strong; she wasn't really doing that much; the bottles were plastic, after all, but Hildy could see that some of them were ruined. Every so often, Molly would open a bottle and fling it. She was already down at the far end of the row.

The swami finally noticed. "Molly," he called. "We can help you, but not if you act like an idiot. What good is that? I agree, Lew shouldn't have done that. You can see what emotions will do, though, can't you? We'll tape up the window…"

Hildy heard more windows breaking; Lew was out of control.

"You'll only destroy yourself that much sooner," the swami called to Molly. "Please. We'll try to help you, Anne and I. And Lew will get himself under control soon. Right, Lew?"

More glass breaking.

Hildy left. They weren't paying much attention to her—which was a surprise. Had Molly started smashing bottles as a diversion, as a way of letting Hildy get out without being noticed? Why would she do that? Hildy's mind was racing, trying to put it all together. Anne certainly had her address, Lew did too. How much pressure could they put on her? And Anne was her chemo nurse! Where could she go without Anne?

She should get some things together and go somewhere else while she figured it all out.

What would happen to Molly? And the book, too; she had left the book behind. But Molly was destroying the time she needed and making it all impossible, really.

She drove back past warehouses, past cars veering down closed alleys and stopping. Were they there to look at the waterfront, or were there other things going on here, strange small dispersions of the norm?

She parked back in Manhattan, trying to walk quickly but efficiently. She didn't want her heart to pound too much, her breath to get too short and sharp. Anne had always counseled steadiness. Don't tire yourself too much; don't push yourself too far. You have drugs in your veins that are affecting your heart, your lungs; be kind.

That's what she'd always said, in her own sweet voice: be kind. Maybe she should go back and ally herself with Anne.

But this business of buying and selling time: was there any way that it would work fairly, once money entered the picture? The acupuncturist, probably a decent man, had started destroying things because he'd promised what he didn't possess and now had thugs at his back. If what he'd said was true.

Commerce in time. It didn't seem right. Though time itself wasn't right, was it, with the way it stopped and started, the way it ran out when you were turning into the person you should be, or even before you were a person, since it ran out on babies, toddlers, teenagers. There was no good system for it. How could you buy and sell time—would you refuse someone who was too poor? Would you keep silent in front of someone who hadn't heard about it?

She felt shame. She had stolen time and used time, even after she'd learned that it was a theft. And she had her own plans, too, plans which now seemed even more urgent. Michael P had been like her, exactly like her, and then he had lost the ability to take the time he needed. Would it happen to her? That felt terrible. A day would come when she would have nothing.

That ached so hard she shivered. If only Noah was alive, if only she could go to him and find relief for a half day, for a few hours, for an hour. Anything to soothe her, just for a while, just to be away from her life as it now was. She thought of him, and the thought was fleeting, it was gone; she desperately needed more.

She would get more. She had a plan.

She bought a gallon of water, emptied out the water, and got some tape and a pen. She taped the jug and wrote Noah's name on it, and a date a year earlier. She drove to Noah's address, parked down the block, and waited until his wife, Eileen, came home. Then she took the jug, went to the house, and rang the bell.

Eileen came to the door. She was tall and thin, and her hair was sprinkled with gray. Good, Hildy thought; she isn't taking care of her appearance yet; she's still grieving.

"I worked with Noah," Hildy said. "I'm sorry to barge in on you, but I was away for a while and I only found out about his death recently, I'm so sorry. He was a wonderful man."

Eileen's eyes looked at her apprehensively.

"It's crazy, I know. I have a gift for you from him. It was a gag gift, supposed to be a gag gift. It was in the closet of his office. I'm sure he forgot about it, or was saving it. I don't know." She let herself trail off indecisively. "May I come in?"

Eileen's eyes had registered surprise and then a keen curiosity. "I'm sorry. I didn't know who you were..." She stepped back and let Hildy in.

The house was neat and surprisingly feminine; she would have expected more austere taste from Noah. There were photos on the wall of Eileen and Noah taken at various vacation spots. There were candid ones of Noah as well, turning to the camera, surprised, in front of a mountain, looking rugged, even one of him with his eyebrows raised and a drink in his hand. He would have hated that one, she thought. This wall was a memorial, then, put up after Noah's death. Hildy had printed out the few photos she had of him on her cell phone and placed them on her own walls. *That* memorial was less official than Eileen's. Eileen had more memories, thick memories, filled with whole days of Noah. That's what Hildy wanted; that's what she needed. Memories of a day with him, waking up with him, eating with him, walking with him, all of it.

Hildy stood there, staring at the photos.

"You said you had something from Noah?" Eileen asked. She was slightly nervous.

Hildy jerked herself away from her thoughts and clutched the bag she'd brought. "I wasn't even sure I should bring it," she said. "It's weird. But it was a year ago. We were celebrating something at the office—I forget what. We had cake and someone had brought balloons. It reminded Carla of an article she'd just read. A woman who had lost her husband came across a balloon in the closet and she remembered that he'd blown it up. She kept it, just thinking about his breath inside that balloon. And then finally, one day when she was feeling low, she pricked it and let his breath wash over her."

Eileen made a small sad sound. "Is that what you have? A balloon?"

"Well, no. We'd used them all up. But we had a gallon of water in the office fridge. Noah dumped it out and said that the balloon couldn't have lasted very long, they always deflate. If a man was going to leave his breath as keepsake, it should be done right. He poured the water out of the jug and let it drain, and then he said, '*This* is how you do it right.' And he took an enormous breath and blew into it and capped it. He put it in the closet, and we all forgot about it."

"You have the jug," Eileen said. Her face had gone pale.

"I have the jug."

They stood there, Eileen swaying slightly, her eyes on the jug as Hildy removed it from the bag. "He wanted that woman to breathe her husband's air," Hildy said. "The air would go into the lungs, and the lungs are next to the heart. That's what he said." She could imagine it; she could almost believe in it. Noah, breath, heart.

"That's Noah," Eileen whispered. She reached out slowly and touched the jug. "His breath," she said. Her voice wavered.

"I didn't know him very well," Hildy said. "We only worked together for a little while, and I just learned about his death. I'm still a little shaken. I'd love to be the one who gave this gift to you, from him, in the way he meant it." She uncapped it, plugging the air inside with her thumb. "Take a deep breath. And I'll pour the air all around you. You'll be surrounded with Noah's breath. Ready?"

Eileen closed her eyes, exhaled, and then inhaled deeply as Hildy whispered, "Now. I'm letting out more air. Now breathe. Now." And as Eileen took her deep breaths, Hildy moved around her, scooping colors, the best colors, the brightest ones, the ones enriched with happiness and Noah. She used everything she'd learned or guessed as she dipped around the inlay of colors, grabbing happiness, strung-together moments, peace and comfort. She filled the jug until the colors back-washed, unable to fit in, and then she capped it.

Eileen had tears running down her face. Her eyes were still closed, her chin was high, her hands were fists.

Was she forgetting? Hildy wondered. Had she already forgotten things? She clutched her jug of Noah memories.

Eileen's face was both radiant and longing. She believed it was Noah's breath; she believed that he was there with her for a moment. But she was merely breathing the ordinary air of her own apartment, which was, in its own way, filled with memories of Noah walking, sitting, looking, smiling.

Hildy's eyes saw the photos on the walls, the windows he had looked out, all of it with the residue of Noah. She could steal memories, but they would be placed within these walls and floors and chairs. Her reveries would include a photo of Eileen in the background, a glance in the mirror with the wrong face looking back; a body that wasn't hers, Noah saying "Eileen" when speaking to her.

It was corrupt. These weren't her memories. And she would know it.

She uncapped the jug, and let the time and memories flow back to Eileen.

Hildy opened the door to her apartment and instantly knew someone was in it. She froze and removed her key gently from the lock. The kitchenette was to her right, so she took a pan off the stove. She walked into her living room and saw through the doorway into her bedroom. She heard a murmur, a very low continuing murmur.

The Bedazzler sat on the edge of the bed, bent over Michael P, who was sprawled on Hildy's bed, looking blankly at the wall.

"She'll get you more time," the Bedazzler murmured into Michael P's ear. Around her were empty jars and bottles. False bottles with nothing in them, Hildy realized, sick to her heart. False bottles placed there after her last fit of pique at yet another break-in.

"I'm sorry," Hildy said. "I'll get time right away."

"Take it from me," the Bedazzler said. "He needs it now. Take it from me."

She glanced at Hildy briefly, just an agonized look, and turned back to Michael P, whispering.

Hildy picked up an empty bottle and turned to the Bedazzler. She swept it behind her head, in a spot she thought was paler, with the future mixed in it, if Molly was correct. "Here," she said, putting her thumb over the mouth of the bottle to keep it from leaking. "Here, take this while I get some more."

The Bedazzler nodded, taking the bottle carefully, putting her own thumb on its mouth, then she laid it against Michael P's mouth. "Breathe, Michael," she whispered. She lifted her thumb a bit, then put it down again. "You have to breathe, Michael, or it will all just go away." She lifted her finger again and even bent closer to blow the time into Michael P's face, but he didn't respond.

"I think—I'm sorry, but I think," Hildy said gently.

"You have to get something better than this," the Bedazzler cried, lifting her finger up completely, letting the time out. Her own time, Hildy realized, and she probably didn't even realize that she was breathing it back in. "This isn't working for him." She took a gulp of the time and opened Michael's mouth and blew it in. His chest rose just a little and then fell back again.

"I think you need to let him sleep," Hildy said, trying to break the Bedazzler's concentration. "I think he won't wake up."

The Bedazzler straightened up, her eyes still on Michael P's face. Which, Hildy thought, had already collapsed a little, the air going out of him. The Bedazzler stared at him. She withdrew the hand she'd laid on his wrist and settled it in her lap. The other hand let the bottle of time go and rested on Michael P's hand. Her body got very still—not quite as still as Michael P's, but quiet and watchful, staring dully at him.

"I didn't understand, you know," Hildy said. "No one explained it to me. No one made it clear."

"And how would anyone explain it," the Bedazzler answered.

Hildy tried again. "Everyone kept breaking in and coming after me. One after the other, trying to get something from me."

"And why wouldn't they," she answered. "Why wouldn't we?"

Her hand held on to Michael P's hand as she added, "And just what did you think you were good for, if not to keep him alive?"

It hit Hildy hard. What indeed was she good for? This great gift she had, this ability to grab time and distribute time—she was wasting it. She might have saved Michael P, she might have saved Rob of the Baldies—indeed, she now realized, in a different way, she might have saved Molly, whose time had been pouring out of windows when she left, who was even now, perhaps, searching the remains for any time that had been left behind.

She drove to Brooklyn, to the warehouse with its shattered bottles of time.

She walked down the aisles with all the overturned crates and smashed bottles. Everyone had left. She went over to the window Molly had kept going to, and she looked out to the two fat cats, and the small parking area with the railing.

She looked down just below and saw a burst of color. The scarf Molly had worn! She ran down and around the building and found Molly propped up against an old dumpster. She was afraid at first that the old woman was dead. But then Molly's head moved just a little, turning to Hildy, and her eyes opened.

"I see you found me," Molly said.

"I found you," Hildy agreed. "I'll call and get help—"

"Wait. I have to give you something. I have to tell you something." She gathered herself as best she could, her right hand shuffling under the edges of her sweater. She brought out the book and put it on her lap and stared at it. "This is everything I know. And Michael P added to it as well, of course." Her eyes latched onto Hildy's eyes and stayed there. "And you'll be next."

Hildy took the book and held it close. "Molly, what do I do?"

"You have to take my time." Her voice was raspy. "Cup by cup," she said. "Take it now. From the left side first. You have to know everything I know, and I'm already too weak to say much." She paused and searched Hildy's face. "Don't hesitate about time. Don't think about it. There's no morality in time, one way or the other. Arbitrary. Unfair. Hideous." She stopped to catch her breath. "Take it all," she said. "Before it's too late." She closed her eyes; her chest rose and fell.

Hildy grabbed jars from her bag. She only had a few, but she scooped out time and put on the caps, and then, with a sense of urgency, she began to scoop out colors and breathe them, and even from within the fuzz of Molly's memories, she scooped out more and breathed in more, as if Molly were directing her from within the time Hildy was taking.

She could almost feel her head swell with Molly's memories. Memories of what she saw mixed in with memories of what Molly saw. She was filling up with time, with Molly's time.

She sat down next to Molly as she slowed down. She had tried to avoid the pearly time, which was small enough, because it was all that was left of Molly's future. But there was so little left! As she sat there, she reached for Molly's hand and held it, feeling it grow cold eventually, its grip relaxed.

It was no small thing to drop Molly's hand and go back to her apartment, pack up all the time she had and rent a hotel room until she could find another place, safe from Anne and the acupuncturist and the guru. She studied the Book of Time carefully, determined to be surgical in her thefts.

She made peace with stealing time. She took it on herself; she accepted the consequences. She would risk being wrong when she stole time or meted it out. She would do it because not doing it was worse.

She did it even as she asked herself how anyone could dare to do it. Make a mistake, and she could take away a life-changing memory, one that could direct a person to greatness, or just great happiness. But to do nothing—to be too weak to take on the guilt—how could she let it continue, that terrible waste? She had been too late to do anything for Michael P, for Rob, for Molly. She would take and she would give, because she could.

If no one took on the burden of stealing time, then no one would reap the benefit of being given time.

There was no justice in time, but occasionally, as she learned hour by hour and day by day —occasionally, there was mercy.

About the Author

Karen Heuler's stories have appeared in over 100 literary and speculative journals and anthologies, from *Alaska Quarterly Review* to *Weird Tales*. She's won an O. Henry award, is frequently nominated for Pushcart and Best American Short Story awards, and was a finalist for the Iowa Short Fiction award, the Bellwether Award, and the Shirley Jackson Award. Her last collection (*Other Places* Aqueduct Press) set women out on adventures throughout the universe.

Visit her website at karenheuler.com